Full Moon at Midnight

David M. Amburgey

"Are they not all ministering spirits, sent out to render service for the sake of those who will inherit salvation?"–Hebrews1:14 NKJV

"I saw visions in my head while on my bed and there was a watcher, a holy one, coming down from heaven."–Daniel 4:13 NKJV

For Brittany, thanks for the inspiration and for letting me use your eyes.

Part 1

"For He shall give His angels charge over you, to keep you in all your ways. In their hands they shall bear you up lest you dash your foot against the stone."–Psalm 91:11-12 NKJV

Chapter One

Darkness besieged her and fear held her in its smothering grip, crushing to the very core of her soul. Her heart raced as if it would leap from her chest, bounding. She stopped to rest, gasping, shoulders heaving. Catching her breath, she leaned against the only tree she found without the low hanging limbs like the others. Those smacked her face as she ran with no regard to her surroundings. With terror-stricken eyes, pupils dilated from pure adrenalin, she searched for an escape, but found none. The break ended, although she had yet to catch her breath; time to run to anywhere but there. The limbs of the trees continued to slap stinging lines across her face. Desperation stung her heart with every whip of the branches.

After a sprint, which seemed to carry her much farther away than she had actually gone, she again stopped to rest, panting. Her large, deep blue eyes stared into the darkness but saw nothing but trees. The full moon gave little light to her cause. The pursuers had grown silent. Maybe she had outrun them. *Maybe they gave up*, she thought. *Riiiight.* Dreaming.

A guttural howl followed by another and a rebel yell awoke her from the musings of her mind. "God, please help me," she cried and ran, stunned with fear and smothered in guilt. Her thoughts raced again.

It seemed a distant memory, but she remembered who she had been, a young lady of good moral standing. She grew up in an excellent family, in a righteous home and in a godly church. She went to church every Sunday and sometimes even on Sunday nights. Although it hadn't been all that long since she went to church, it all seemed to another lifetime. It seemed in that church had become just a ritual to her, as if she were not there at all. Her mind wandered: boys, school and school activities, what she planned to do that weekend, or other distractions in life. Her morality was still intact, but her walk with God had strayed. Things of life took precedence for her, and things of the eternal nature were no longer thought of at all. She lived in the moment. She lived for herself.

She again stopped running, helpless and exhausted. She knew she must continue and concentrate on her escape, but her thoughts would not fix upon but one thing, guilt.

I'll change, God. This time I mean it and will go to be with you and because you are there, not just because my parents make me. I will even tell others about you, Lord. Just don't let these demons kill me. She looked down at her hands, which shook from the combination of fear and pure exhaustion. *I'm so afraid. Please, God, don't let me die.* God had heard a prayer similar to this one too many times, just not from her, until now. Most would forget as soon as the distressing time has gone away.

But God heard her cry, *"God, please help me,"* as did the one who, along with God, had always been there, her Watcher.

***

Tiffany's Watcher first arrived on earth nearly a year prior to her birth, as was the norm, but she came two months earlier than expected. Her time in the neonatal intensive care unit would have been a scary time for any child. Imagine. The first thing that you see in this world is a foreign environment and strange faces, which would shock enough, but add to that these strange large beings prodding and poking you all about. Painful objects being poked into you; tubes shoved into your nose and mouth. *What is this place? What are they doing to me? Why? It was so warm and so much nicer inside.* Naturally, fear and confusion would consume this child.

The Watcher held her tiny little premature hand and whispered the assurance to her that everything would be alright soon. She just had to stay in her little box, incubator, for a little longer and develop her lungs a bit more so that she could go home.

He showed up again when she broke her arm at six. She was climbing a magnificent tree when she plummeted to the ground. Her watcher broke the rules. "Just this once, Lord," he said, and took on a solid, human form so that he could carry her to safety.

The ruling Angels of heaven would consider this to be a serious transgression, and the Watcher had to explain his reasoning for it. It was an unwritten but well-known rule amongst the angels that those assigned to a person only watched and guided them in secret or without being seen. Except in times of extreme emergency, such as premature death. They were to only watch and to guide, unbeknownst to their subjects. It often left them helpless and frustrated, but it allied itself with their greatest rule: Never influence the free will of humanity.

***

Tiffany's Watcher again stood with her, ready to fight for her and even give the greatest sacrifice of all for her, if need be.

"Let me help her, God, just this…" Tiffany's Watcher, Victor, paused in his prayer with the memory of the last time he used the phrase, "Just this once." Gabriel had given him a scolding unparalleled by any other and told him to never reveal himself to any human again. And since then, he hadn't. *But wouldn't this be an 'extreme emergency?'* More of a prayer than a thought.

Victor's memory clung to the last time that he broke this rule.

"Your job is to watch and to protect," Gabriel admonished. "They are never to know that you are with them. Watch them, care for them, and even love them, which is a part of our nature, but always from the spiritual realm. To reveal one's self to a human is a great breach of protocol." He ended his reprimand of righteous indignation by storming out of the room and saying, "Never let it happen again. This is your warning, Victor. If it happens again, you will face a reassignment or worse, grounded." Victor recoiled from Gabriel's reaction. He couldn't imagine getting the same reprimand from Michael. He shuddered at the thought. And he didn't want to be grounded. For a watcher to be grounded is the ultimate humiliation. Why, for an angel to be stripped of his wings...

Reassigned! Grounded?! But I would rather die than to leave her. I, I love her. This little jewel of beauty had quite taken him from the time that he first met her, not long after her birth. He couldn't help but to be taken by her sparkling, big and beautiful blue eyes. She didn't have her golden hair then, or her little dimples when she smiled, which made her so adorable. The older she got, the more beautiful she became; her inner beauty, her spark. It is a part of a young lady that young boys take for granted because they often only see what is on the surface or the outside. Deep within, her eyes held a certain glow, one that just showed her wonderful soul.

Victor shook his thoughts back to the problem at hand. *Focus, Victor!*

If I help her again, I will lose her, but if I don't, she will die. Either way, I will lose her. And she will never know... she will never know. The actual truth: she would never know that he even existed. It is the greatest pain every watcher felt; unrequited love. His mind wandered again.

———

He had a discussion with one of his fellow watchers once while they sat upon a cloud gazing down at the Grand Canyon. The clouds often provided the best view around. Victor felt guilty for how he adored this beautiful young creature, and his friend told him not to worry. It came naturally to them. "We all love them," he shrugged. "In reality, it's a part of our directive, and the one part of our job that is the most difficult. Yet we love them just the same. Even when they move to their glorious reward, we just get assigned to another to watch over, and then another and another, and this will continue until the end of time. Or if you are fortunate enough like me, you become a mentor to someone like you and that has its own rewards. Then, at the end of time..." he shrugged, "who knows, maybe we will meet them all. They will know of our existence then."

"B-but, can't we love too much? I mean, there has to be a limit... a barrier, right? I adore this young human and everything about her." Both knew that the infatuation, the love, which Victor and all watchers shared for their subjects, was the deepest kind of love, having nothing at all to do with physical attraction, but a type of love not so easy to explain or dismiss.

His more seasoned friend and mentor laughed, "There is never a limit on love, my friend, and nobody can ever love too much; only not enough. The way you love her just says that you are a good watcher. She is fortunate to have one who loves her so much. As for the barrier, the answer to that lies in our mandates." Patting Victor on the back, he got up to leave. "Hang in there. This is your first assignment, and we never forget the first. Those," he stretched, "are the ones that we love the most. Just be careful not to break the rules, and remember, it is her life and she must make her own choices, even if that choice is ignorant or wrong. You can put things in their path, guide them, suggest things in their dreams or whatever way you can think of to aid them, but with humans we must always honor their free will. That is Father's greatest rule."

"Yes," Victor stared at the Grand Canyon as he sighed, "I know." Then he lowered his voice, "but I would die for her."

"We all would if we could," The voice of Victor's mentor, Raul, came from the distance; echoed, "but we can't die unless we reveal ourselves in the flesh. That must only be in a time of dire need and a last resort. If that time ever comes, you will know it. Besides, someone has already died for them, so there is no more need for death. Not from us. All they have to do is accept Him. In that, their death on earth doesn't matter, for then they will only transform into a greater existence." Victor was alone, but his mentor's voice remained. "Goodbye Victor, I have the funeral of a godly man to attend. Those are always joyous occasions, though sad for some, and watchers always need a little extra help."

———

I would die for her. A bone-chilling howl interrupted Victor's thought, whipping him from the memory to the problem at hand. He saw Tiffany, gasping for air and struggling to distance herself from her pursuers. *But I can't. If I pick her up and carry her off, I will lose her forever. If I don't, these who chase her will catch her and devour her, their intent being to end her life.*

"What choice do I have, Father," he looked up, speaking into the abyss of. "I can't let her die. She's only sixteen and has a long life ahead of her. She will get married; have kids; become a grandma. It will be a beautiful life because she is a wonderful soul. Don't let her die from this one mistake." As an answer to Victor's prayer, a cloud rolled from covering the full moon and everything came into sight.

Tiffany had again stopped, her lungs begging for relief, she could not go much further. Victor struggled with what he knew he must do. *Don't give up, Tiffany,* he thought. "Run!" He cried, knowing that she couldn't hear him. He could see deep into Tiffany's once bright blue eyes, now pale-gray with fear.

Although exhausted beyond measure, she ran toward a clearing, a road which she had seen as the light glistened from the full moon. "That's my girl," Victor smiled, *run.* She ran with pure desperation; adrenalin. She ran on fumes.

***

The howls, yells and carried by the soft breeze, eviscerated a moment of silence, drew closer. Victor eyed those who made chase, back to Tiffany, and back to them. *They will catch her soon.* His fear forced a decision. *Run my little fawn,* he thought, *run like clouds roll through the sky... run like you have never run before. The hunters draw near and you must make it to the river and plunge in where they will no longer have your scent.*

In Victor's point of view, time seemed to slow for Tiffany and everything around her moved quickly as she proceeded. "Run!!" he cried, but she still could not hear him.

He surveyed the situation again. *They're getting closer. I can't watch her die, I just can't. I must stop them.* Then an idea struck him. *I may not reveal myself to her, but nothing in my training ever said that I couldn't reveal myself to them. It is a part of my edict to protect her, to protect one of God's chosen few.* He smiled as he watched Tiffany run away in desperation, knowing that all would be okay. *She will get away.* He shrugged. *And I will face another inquiry.* "It's worth it," he chuckled. As he turned to her pursuers, who had yet to make it to where he stood, he spread his wings as far as they would stretch and he glowed with the splendor that God had given him as a creature of heaven. He thought a lone word into the void of time and space as he prepared for battle: "Help!" Then, revealing himself to those who chased his beloved Tiffany, he roared with what angels liked to call "the Voice of God." Although a far cry from the actual voice of God, it got the point across, "THIS IS AS FAR AS YOU GO, DEMONS AND WORSHIPERS OF DEMONS!"

Tiffany slowed as she glanced back to see the position of the pursuers. The woods filled with an illuminating presence. In that moment she knew she would be safe, and she voiced that knowledge with one word.

Somehow, she knew the source of that blinding glow, but also knew that she shouldn't have known it or his name. Knowing it gave her peace and the feeling of euphoria. The flash in her eyes returned them from gray to blue as joy poured over her, as she whispered his name with a smile, "Victor."

Confident in her safety, she walked away.

Chapter Two

Several Days Earlier

"Are you going to the party Friday night? It's the biggest party of the year, you know. Everybody's going to be there. Well, everybody who is anybody anyway, and losers too. There are always losers, you know." Kessie gazed at Tiffany, who attempted to ignore her. "You must come." She continued in her whiny, begging voice, coupled with a pouty lip and big brown puppy dog eyes. It worked on the guys and Kessie's parents, but not Tiffany.

"I don't think so," Tiffany replied without even looking up at her friend. "You know I don't do the party thing. There is always drinking," she added an inflection of disgust to her voice, "and drugs. Pot. I hate that stuff and don't care to be anywhere near it."

"Pot?!" Kessie laughed, "Oh it's harmless."

"It stinks. Why would anyone smoke something that stinks? Like smoking dog poo. And don't get me started on the alcohol, it just turns people into idiots." She raised her hands and twisted her face in disgust, "Oh, and, then you puke everywhere. Yeah, some real fun there."

"I smoke pot and drink some."

Tiffany mustered a smile and said with the wave of her hand, "Exhibit A, your honor."

That's my girl, Victor thought as he sat in the short distance, taking part in his favorite pastime, watching Tiffany. Pride swelled in him. No one could see him. The best way to watch is when no one noticed you watching? If you are watching and get caught, you would have to stop with awkward embarrassment.

The teen years were so important for everyone. Young ladies like Tiffany in particular, Victor thought he should hang around closer than usual. He used that as an excuse, but he wouldn't miss a moment because he adored her and found nothing more interesting or gratifying than hanging around with Tiffany. Besides, what if something happened while he wandered off somewhere doing something else? Then he would have to drop everything to come running to his girl. Angels have many powers, but omnipresence is not one of them. So, he watched.

"*He'll* be there, and *he'll* have his shirt off." Kessie continued to tempt and knew who to use as her vessel for temptation; the one boy in school who had caught Tiffany's eye, Jason. "Don't you just love those six-pack abs and that carved chest?" she asked, staring off into the void with a dreamy expression. "Mmm!" Tiffany looked up as Jason passed by and gave her a quick wink. She couldn't help but smile and blush a little. Kessie barely noticed, but she noticed, "Mmm, mmm, tasty. He is soooo hot." She pushed Tiffany on the shoulder. "He likes you and I know you just loooove him."

As Tiffany stared at him, she remembered the first time they had met several weeks before. Gym class. Of course, Kessie, like a cat, noticed him and his abs before anyone when he removed his shirt while he entered the boys' locker room. She pointed it out to Tiffany. And, again, like a cat in heat, she threw herself at him when he came out of the locker room. He was a strong pillar, immoveable; immune to Kessie's charm. Instead, he walked over to Tiffany. "HI, I'm Jason, and who is this before me whom I have the privilege of meeting?" His smile enthralled her.

"Tiffany," was all she could muster to say behind a shy smile and flushed skin. Her eyes gleamed when she smiled. Hiding her excitement proved difficult. This guy, cute and nice and didn't fall for Kessie's tricks. Every boy, or so it seemed, fell for Kessie's tricks. Many pined for Tiffany and she played hard to get, so they often settled for Kessie. Of course, someone as beautiful and as pure-hearted as Tiffany could afford to be choosy. Kessie held great beauty in her own right, but when compared to Tiffany, like most young ladies, she paled in comparison. Most of them lacked that special something; a spark.

Jason proved to be a gentleman. He could have been an utter

jerk and Tiffany wouldn't have noticed, as his allure had her from the beginning. But he had the looks, and the charm, with it. Tiffany thought she had found the perfect guy, and that is saying a lot.

"Go away! Leave me alone," she told Kessie and continued to smile while snapping out of her memory.

"Be there; you guys can hook up." Kessie looked up at Jason again as he sat at a table by himself. "Tough being the new guy, but mmm, he'll have no problem with popularity, at least with us girls, anyway. Girl, I'd go after him myself, but I see how he looks at you. I can't compete against your big blue eyes. None of us can. When you're around, we don't stand a chance, and girl, he has already noticed you. It's too late for any of us." Tiffany looked up and again caught Jason's gaze. She blushed and graced him with her contagious smile. He smiled back with a perfect smile. "See, I told you girl." Kessie continued and ended with a sigh as she rested her chin in her hand and wished that Jason would see her in the same way. "You know, I think he's got to be perfect."

As Kessie prattled in a mindless rampage that faded into Tiffany's thoughts, Tiffany contemplated on what she had said, but kept her thoughts to herself, *go after him yourself, humph, you would go after any guy as long as he had a pulse. Besides,* she looked at her with some disdain as she continued to gab in ignored silence; *you went after him and he shut you down.* She allowed herself a sly smile, which led to a brighter smile as she caught Jason watching her again. He walked over to the table where the girls sat. Tiffany's heart raced.

"He's coming over here, girl." Kessie stated the obvious out of the side of her mouth, interrupting herself. She popped her head up from her hand and then continued when Jason got closer. "Hi Jason, you settling in to the new school and all?" She smiled so fake it made her gums shine more than her teeth.

Jason nodded, "Yeah," he didn't take his eyes off of Tiffany for a moment. He cleared his throat.

That's so sweet, Tiffany thought, *he's nervous.*

"Um," he cleared his throat again, "Tiffany?"

"Yes?" She smiled again; it came so naturally to her. Her smile, true and warm, melted the hearts of many young boys and men of all ages. *Spit it out already,* she thought as her smile faded. She caught herself and, while cocking her head to the side, she squinted and resumed her previous pose.

"Going to the party Friday?" Jason asked.

Victor, who had preoccupied himself with other thoughts, snapped to and gulped. *No!* He thought, *she will not go. What are you doing, you colossal idiot? You'll ruin everything. She doesn't need to be around that party trash. If I could, I'd cream you myself, you stupid little punk.* He drew closer, furrowing his brow, gazing at Jason as if to intimidate. *Tell him, Tiffany. You want nothing to do with this.* He continued to stare. He sneered at Jason, drawing so close to his face that he could smell his breath. When he got really close to him, Jason took one step back as he awaited Tiffany's answer. *Why did he step back?* Victor thought, astonished. *Could he sense me?* He, too, recoiled in surprise.

"Are you? I mean..." she replied, flustered.

"I'll go if you go," he put his hand on the back of his head, a nervous habit, "I guess what I am saying is," he sighed, "I'd like to be your escort for the evening."

Tell him no. Victor scoffed.

She smiled and blushed again. "Ok."

That's my girl... wait? What? The shock of Tiffany's rapid response stunned Victor.

Tiffany didn't want to go, but agreeing with Jason seemed too easy. It even surprised her she agreed so quickly. What made this guy so special? Good looking and polite. He seemed so... mature. She thought, *I mean, who says things like escort for the evening? Lame... but cute.* His sweet approach increased her attraction toward him.

Victor brimmed with grief and near rage, because he could do nothing. Tiffany had chosen to say yes. He didn't want her to go, but he had no way of stopping her. Maybe she will get bored and talk him into leaving early. Maybe she will talk him into doing something else altogether. Victor trusted Tiffany. She would make the right choice. *Yeah,* he thought, trying to convince himself, *she'll do the right thing. She always does.* Victor had some work to do.

What will I tell my parents? Tiffany thought. *They will make me stay home if they find out that it is a party and how big of a party it is.*

The bell rang.

As they got up to leave, Jason smiled, gave Tiffany another wink and said, "Well, okay, then. I guess I'll see you on Friday." By then Kessie faded into the shadows. Present yet invisible. Jason chanced putting a hand on Tiffany's back, just below the neck. A gesture of easing her before him and when she didn't resist, he left his hand there for a moment or two. "Can I walk you to your next class?"

Wow, she thought again, *he's so sweet. Most guys just follow me to my class, but he asked. Wow.* She smiled, "Uh, sure, but won't you be late for class?" He nodded, shrugged, and smiled as they walked down the hall.

Victor followed, grumbling. He didn't know what, but there was just something about Jason he didn't like. Jealousy? Maybe, but it seemed much more.

Chapter Three

The afternoon flew by like the fog from a night of dreams. She heard nothing in her classes, gazed off into nowhere, and thought about Jason. Of spending time with him and getting to know him better. Wondering what he would be like and reasoned that he would be a pure gentleman. She sighed and continued on her afternoon journey through reverie.

She had one problem, however; she had to figure out how to convince her parents to let her go.

Late that afternoon, Tiffany still hadn't thought of a way to get around her problem. She planned to date a guy that her parents didn't know and that she didn't know very well. If the truth came out, they would give a quick and emphatic "No!" and it would be in stereo. Done! Over!

There had to be a way to tell them she wanted to go Friday and not let on where they will be. For as long as she could remember, Tiffany hadn't lied to her parents and didn't want to start now, but if she wanted to go out with Jason, there didn't seem to be any other choice.

As she had done many times since childhood, Tiffany found her place of solitude, which was a small corner on the back deck of their house next to the pool in the backyard. This was where she went to think. The place provided comfort, shade, and a place to hide. Even on a hot summer's day it was a good place to get away from everyone and everything, if even for but a moment. The personal time would always end the same way. With her mother calling for her for several minutes, then her coming out to the back deck and peeking around the small corner where the deck wrapped around the screened-in porch. "Didn't you hear me calling you?" she would always ask.

Tiffany's life at home didn't differ from many others. She had two younger brothers and a little sister, Emily, the youngest who got anything that she wanted. Tiffany had the unfortunate stigma of being the oldest, so, as she saw it anyway, she didn't get to do anything she wanted.

Her dad kept her on a short leash. He exercised great wisdom as a father of a beautiful young lady at Tiffany's age, but it often seemed to be a little overbearing. Not that he didn't trust her, or that he wished to dominate her during the most impressionable time of her life. He didn't trust any of the young boys that she would bring home for him to meet. He remembered being that age and knew how the minds of young teenage boys worked, especially with girls as beautiful as Tiffany.

Victor often agreed with Tiffany's father on what she could do and where she could go. A young lady didn't need to "Traipse around, flaunting herself or putting on a show, and if a young man had half the scruples that he should, then he would agree." That was one of the many things Tiffany tired of hearing from her father.

None of the boys would ever be good enough for his daughter: too skinny, too cocky, too dumb (his favorite), too old, or just too ugly. "You can do better than that guy." Another sentiment Victor agreed with. He couldn't have found a better dad for Tiffany if he chose the man himself.

Her mother loosened a little more because she remembered being sixteen and also had a dad that she thought didn't let her do anything. Goes with the territory.

The social life of Tiffany often arose in conversations between her mother and father. Her mother would talk her father into letting her go to some functions, even if he had refused. He would even try to put his foot down sometimes, but the mother always got her way. If mom said it was okay, then it often remained that way.

Now, if Tiffany's mother said "no", then that was it. Her dad tried to reverse the roles once in a while and tried to play the advocate for Tiffany and sweet talk mother into changing her mind, but always to no avail.

Tiffany sat in her little corner and ran all the scenarios and outcomes through her head. It would be a hard sell, being honest and telling her parents, and she knew it. She didn't like the outcome of the scenarios involving the truth as they rolled through her mind, even if they downplayed the size of the party. *Why did I say yes?* She thought. *Why hadn't I said that I would tell him tomorrow?* She knew that if she told her parents the truth, no matter how she put it, they would make her stay home. The worst part of it lived in her, telling Jason that she couldn't go. That would be devastating.

After over half an hour in her place of solitude, she went inside. She decided that the only way to make things right in this situation was to lie. She felt she had no other choice.

***

While Tiffany sat in her private spot, Victor joined her, sitting on the edge of the deck rail, watching. He knew her so well that he could almost read her thoughts. As a watcher, another unwritten rule in not breaking the free will of God's beloved children existed: let them to keep their thoughts to themselves. Victor couldn't block the strong thoughts that came screaming out because of the force in which they presented themselves. These thoughts often held dominant emotion, deep contemplation or conviction, and often premeditated sins.

When Tiffany went inside, Victor heard one word in his mind with a painful, yet clear pang, "LIE!"

When a child of God plans something wrong, it emits with prominent emotion. The mind broadcasts it all around because the person is so focused on the thought. It resonated as an almost subconscious cry for help and wreaked of desperation. In these situations, the watcher feels compelled to stop the action from occurring. Victor would do everything in his power, short of revealing himself and warning his subject to stop, to keep her from going through with what she planned to do. God gave watchers to his children to watch over them and keep them out of trouble, and if the need arose, to ensure that they would not make a mistake that could follow them for the rest of their lives, cost them their lives, or worse, their eternal separation from God. Tiffany intended to make one of those mistakes that might put her on a path that could end in destruction, and Victor would do everything in his power to stop it.

Chapter Four

Several hours later, the family gathered around the supper table. It was one of Victor's favorite times to visit with Tiffany. He loved the smell of the food and how it all looked at the table, organized like the picture in a magazine. He wished to eat some of it. *That would be divine,* he thought. Before they ate, each one in the family bowed their heads and the dad asked one of them to lead in the blessing over the food.

Mitchell, the second to the youngest child and the youngest boy, always gave stirring sermonette prayers that made his watcher proud.

The family often indulged in idle conversation at the table. "How was your day? What did you do at school today? How did you do on the Math test?" That sort of thing. Dad's work would come up or some political goings on around the world that Tiffany couldn't care less about because it just didn't fit into her little sixteen-year-old world. If it wasn't on social media, about cheer camp, boys, or one of her TV shows, then she didn't care.

In times past she feigned interest, but on that night she didn't bother. Her mind still focused on her dilemma. Victor could still hear the thought resonating from her loud and clear. It came through to him so strongly that it hurt. Tiffany just sat there and stared at her plate, pushing her vegetables around with the fork.

"Are you alright, Tiffany?" Her mother interrupted the uncommon silence, but Tiffany didn't answer, so she called her name again.

"Huh? Oh, yeah, just thinking." She took a deep breath and dove right through the open door and began with her lie. "A guy has asked me out this weekend."

Oh, no, Victor thought, *I have to stop this.* When little Emily reached up for her glass to take a drink, Victor seized the opportunity and knocked the glass over, spilling its contents all over her side of the table, and the juice dripped onto the floor. A symphony of chaos resulted. Mitchell and his brother screamed. Emily stared at the spilled contents in shock with a look on her face that said, "Oops, I didn't mean to."

"Pick up the tablecloth, Mitchell, so it won't get any more on the floor," mother said. She ran into the kitchen for some towels. Mitchell understood; this was not the first time someone spilled something at that table and it wouldn't be the last. The mom returned within seconds to clean up the mess. "Oh, Emily, be more careful."

"It wasn't my fault, Mommy, it just slipped. I got butter on my fingers, see." She smiled a wide grin, which revealed that her two front teeth were missing, and held up her fingers for everyone to see. Her dad chuckled at the statement, and her mother smiled. Tiffany stared in awe while waiting for the moment to end so that she could continue with the conversation that she had started earlier.

"Yes, I know, honey," her mother said as she continued to clean up the mess. "now wipe off your hands and be more careful," she softly scolded Emily.

Tiffany giggled, but sneered inside because she knew that if it had been anyone else, butter on their fingers or not, they would have gotten into trouble. One boy would have mouthed back and the mom would have sent him to his room; not for spilling, but for mouthing off.

It took a few minutes to clean up the mess and get everything settled down enough for everyone to return to their meal and the previous conversation. Tiffany didn't miss a beat, for as soon as it was possible to do so, she continued, breaking the silence in the aftermath, "I've already told him yes." She didn't look up from her plate and her father, with a mouthful of food in his cheek, stopped, set down his fork and stared at her.

Victor scanned the room to find anything else that would distract from this conversation, hoping, given the opportunity to think, Tiffany would change her mind and be honest about the matter. He had to think fast because Tiffany had determined to lie, and she thought of something that would convince them.

Victor became desperate, and his mind settled on something in the next room. Just through the opening to the dining room, he thumped the light bulb on the lamp closest to them. With a flash and a slight pop, the den darkened, and it startled everyone enough to turn their attention to the other room.

The dad went over to the cabinet to get a light bulb and changed it. This brief distraction didn't take as long as Victor hoped. Before Tiffany's father had even gotten back to his seat, he continued the conversation himself and it went similarly to every conversation of this nature. "Do we know this boy?"

"No, he's new." She continued to stare at her plate and push her food around on it.

All Victor could hear in his mind was, "LIE! LIE! LIE! LIE! LIE!" It grew more prominent and much louder the closer Tiffany got to it. He had become frantic to find something, anything, to keep this conversation from continuing.

"Do we know his parents?"

"No, sir, but…"

"No. No buts. If we don't know him, his parents, or anything about him, then the answer is going to be no."

"But I've already told him yes." She said in a whiney voice. She looked at her father with a bit of disgust. Her face darkened red, half from anger and half from the thought of the embarrassment this would bring her. "It will humiliate me if I have to tell him."

"Well, whose fault is that?" Her father replied, "Not mine." His voice raised as he showed his impatience with the conversation. Mother placed her hand on his arm in a calming gesture and looked at him. She said a mouthful in the simple gaze without having to say a word. He sighed.

"Where are you going and who will be there?" The mother

turned her attention to Tiffany; her hand still on the father's arm. He held a sour look and was flush with anger.

Tiffany sighed in the attempt to calm herself. She still fought the battle. Honesty had been her way with everyone, her parents most of all. *This is the reason it will work.* The thought was so evil and sudden that it shocked her, but she agreed it made sense.

"LIE! LIE! LIE! LIE!" It grew louder, louder, LOUDER in Victor's mind, and he scrambled to keep his beloved Tiffany from getting into this trap that the devil or one of his demons had set for her. *Uh, uhm, think, Victor, think! An earthquake, no, not that. Besides, I don't have that kind of power. I mean I could if I went beneath the surface, found a fault line and move some rocks around, but there's no time for that. A fire... no, that's stupid. Yeah, you big dummy, just kill them all trying to save Tiffany from a lie. Mm,* his mind whirled while trying to find something to stop this from happening. And then it was too late. Before he could react, Tiffany spewed the lie from her mouth.

"Heather and her boyfriend and Jason and I thought we would go out to eat and a late movie. We will be back by midnight curfew, I promise." Tiffany changed her look to her cute and innocent little girl facade that often worked with all men and tossed a smile at her dad, turning on the charm. It didn't work for her mother, but it often did for her dad. Men are suckers for a pretty face and a smile. At least she didn't pull out the tears.

Victor stood there in shock, shaking his head as it hung low. He had failed to stop the deed. Tiffany had made her choice. She would have to pay the price, because every sin has its consequences; he just hoped that it wouldn't be anything that may bring lasting harm to his beloved girl.

Tiffany had chosen the perfect lie. Heather was a good one to choose because her dad adored Heather about as much as he did his own daughter. She was in the Sunday school class that he taught, and he considered her to be a delightful girl. As for Heather's boyfriend, the lie couldn't have been more perfect. He went to their church too and was also in the same Sunday school class. They were both senior and responsible, more than most people their age.

The dining room fell silent. Tiffany's parents held a conversation with each other by looking at each other and not saying a word. All Victor could think was *please say no, please say no...* He even clinched his eyes shut and repeated the phrase, attempting to insert the thought into her dad's mind. *Maybe if I stand up straight and tap my heels together...*

Placing a thought was something that Victor could not do, except, maybe, in a dream. God only gave that special ability to the Messenger angels. The only way to get a signal to the mind of another was through the Holy Spirit. To the great displeasure of Victor, the silence broke.

"I guess it will be ok as long as Heather and Mike chaperons you guys."

Tiffany jumped up from her chair and ran over to her father, saying, "Oh, thank you, Daddy, thank you." She wrapped her arms around him and gave him a big kiss on the cheek.

"Alright, alright," he smiled while pushing her away, "go sit down and eat your supper." He looked up, pointing a finger at her, "Tell that boy to come early so I can meet him." Tiffany nodded in agreement.

When Tiffany sat back down, she ate her supper while telling her family how cute, tall and how much of a gentleman Jason was; how every girl thought he was so great, and that she was lucky he chose her. On and on, she rambled. None of them wanted to hear any of it, especially her dad and Victor, but they indulged her excitement as she babbled about how excited she was to go out with this boy. Her brothers made a few snide comments, to which Tiffany only replied to with a sneer.

It was Wednesday night, so they all went to church. In the teen group meeting, she didn't listen. All she could think about was Jason, how good he looked, and how awesome it would be to go out with him. This, she thought, could be the beginning of an amazing relationship. The youth leader at her church taught on peer pressure, focusing on doing things we wouldn't otherwise because of it. Then he went into how they, through the power of God in their lives, could remain above the influence. It was a spot-on lesson for Tiffany. Unfortunately, she hadn't heard a word. Victor, who sat behind her, sulking from his failure, didn't listen either.

Chapter Five

High above the earth, Victor sat upon a cloud looking down at the Amazon River, moping. After a brief period on the cloud, he sensed the familiar presence of his old mentor, Raul. He looked up from the hypnotizing view of the winding river below. "Hello, Raul. Thanks for coming."

"No problem, my friend. I had a moment or two. Is your girl still sleeping?"

He nodded. "Then she has school. This early they are less likely to stir up too much trouble. But I can be there in an instant."

When Victor was in training with his old mentor, the mighty Watcher Angel Raul, and before he graduated from the academy and released to go on to his first assignment, Raul pulled him aside and set up a signal to use whenever he needed to talk. No "Angel Signal" lamp that put angel wings in the sky or anything like that existed. Angels can communicate in more ways than humans. All they have to do is link with their minds. If one pushed hard enough, they could form a strong link that would be uncomfortable for both. Like humans, Angels would rather have no one else be in their heads except the Holy Father.

A specific code word had to be set up between comrades so that one would not block out the other. All Victor had to do was to think one word and send it, "Cloud." "Help," was also a signal word, but that would broadcast to all and show a dire need.

When this word entered the mind, then one would look for the other sitting on a cloud somewhere above the world. It is not as difficult as it seems. Angels can search every cloud in the world quickly from high above; one of the many advantages of having a wingspan wider than their already exorbitant height and their vision was much enhanced.

Often, when the two of them sat on a cloud, they would remember old times. On this occasion, Victor chose the memory to review.

"What kind of name is Raul for an Angel, anyway?" Victor smiled, remembering the first time he had met Raul, eons before. He was a young, wet behind the ears Angeling who knew nothing about anything. He just knew that they assigned him to be a Watcher angel, and an angel named Raul was to be his trainer.

***

(Understanding Angels - lesson 1)

Angels live forever, but they have not all existed from the beginning. The more the population of the earth grows, more angels become necessary. Each child of God that will give themselves to Him and accept the Christ gets a watcher angel at the time of his or her birth.

If you wonder how God and the Angel academy know who will or who will not give his heart to Christ, the answer to that is simple. God is God, and He knows everything. From the beginning to the end, He knows it all. It is easy for Him to know who will or who will not give their life to Him because He sees it. Of course, this presents another difficulty for the Watchers because they cannot force the will of God upon the Children of God. They must choose on their own. This is especially frustrating for some, because many do not accept the Savior until moments before death.

God knows who will or will not find salvation and when, but angels do not. Of course, it is His will for all to give their allegiance to Him, but He knows that for just as many who choose to love Him and give their lives to Him, an equal or greater amount will choose not to.

Spreading the gospel message to the world is the job of Christians. There were times long ago when Angels brought messages to humanity, but those times have long since passed. The Messenger Angels all have it easy and have supervisory roles.

Watcher Angels do all the work on earth.

***

Raul roared with laughter at the memory evoked by Victor's comment. He remembered with much joy their first meeting. Victor was a cocky Angeling who thought he could do anything, take on anyone, and had something to prove to everyone. He shook his head, laughing, and responded the same way he had long ago, "And what kind of name is Victor for an angel?"

"Touché," Victor said. Both of them laughed.

———

The young Angeling got perturbed at Raul, worked himself into a fit of rage and tried to rush at him. *He's old. I can take him,* he thought. Raul stepped aside, nudging Victor, allowing his own weight and momentum to carry him to the ground with a sickening thud. Victor didn't see it, but Raul winced.

Raul gave the young Angeling his first of many lessons in combat, and life itself. "Now, why are you on the ground?"

In response, Victor got up. Still blinded by rage, he charged again with the same results. Raul turned toward the young Angel who was again lying with his face on the ground, "Again I ask, 'Why are you on the ground?'" Victor huffed from fatigue and stared at his new mentor with contempt while trying not to topple over. Raul stood ready for the next rush, but unlike before, Victor contemplated the question.

Raul continued, "Were you on the ground because I am faster than you, or stronger? Or was it your rage that got the best of you?" He paused for effect, letting the thought sink in. "You must remember, never let your emotions get the best of you. When left unchecked, they will destroy you or at least cause you to plant yourself face first on the ground."

"Yes, master," he replied, humbled. He bowed low, giving allegiance to his new mentor and trainer with the name that didn't befit an angel. Now, he had also learned that day that neither did his name.

———

"So," Raul interrupted the memory, "why is it you have called me to this cloud? If I recall the last time, you called upon me, the young lady was six and you were in quite a confused state after rescuing her from a fall and you had made the choice to reveal yourself to her." He paused and laughed to himself, "Something about loving too much, I believe."

Victor smiled. "A wise old angel with a funny name once told me that one can never love too much." He lowered his head and shook it before continuing with a sigh and a slight smile, which he aimed at Raul. "Will there ever be a day when my training with you will end?"

"Ha ha," he threw his head back, "I suppose there never will, my friend. There is always something new to learn. The moment that we learn it all, or at least think that we have, the Good Master throws a pop quiz."

"I'm worried." Victor spat it out, ready to tell why he had summoned Raul to the cloud. "I tried to stop it, but she was so persistent in continuing with it no matter what. I tried creating a mess, blowing a light bulb. I even thought about setting the kitchen on fire, but no matter what I did, she had determined to go ahead with it. It was a lie," he continued, his face showing his dismay, "the most insignificant of the sins, yet the deadliest of them all." Victor did not turn his gaze from the Amazon River basin. He stared at it, but his focus was much closer, deep within his own mind.

"Yes," Raul said, leaning on the cloud, "the lie could well be the worst of them all. A lie is never alone. It always leads to something else, and to more lies. When they fall into the trap of lies, it grows into a monster that can prove impossible to contain or ward off. It always brings harm even when they escape the trap. If they don't confess and change, and do so quickly, it will destroy them in the end. To humans it is small. When a lie is told that small seed grows into an ominous weed and then it grows out of control. As it spreads and grows, it will reach a point where it will eventually contaminate everything that is good within them. Satan is the Father of Lies, so it only makes sense that a lie would be his mightiest of weapons."

"But, what can I do?" Victor asked. "She has already set in motion a chain reaction that could destroy her life and maybe even her soul. How do I stop the repercussions; things that her actions have already set into motion?"

Victor received extensive training in battle and in the art of cunning, or coercing people into doing good deeds or avoiding bad ones without direct interference. They taught him about all the sins that people would commit and how to defend and battle against them. He could ward off demons with the flick of the wrist; keep the principalities and powers off of Tiffany forever if he must. He could even help keep her from certain types of sin, but once a lie is told, once they commit a sin, his recourse remains limited. All the power vested in him by the Almighty Father and the training from the Watcher Academy becomes useless once the lie was told. He knew that, but hoped Raul knew some trick that he had yet to teach him. Something that would help Tiffany get out of this trap and to avoid the consequences.

"I'm afraid, my friend," Raul gave Victor a solemn look and patted him on the back as he leaned forward in preparation to stand, "that there is nothing you can do. Once the lie is told, it cannot be untold. What they have done, we cannot undo. The outcome is in motion, the penalty has already begun and there is nothing that you, I or anyone else in all of God's creation can do to stop it. I'm afraid she will have to pay the price for her transgression; it is the oldest and most holy law. She can confess, yes, and yes, Christ gave His life for her so that she wouldn't have to die in her sin, but if she sins after accepting him and His sacrifice, even when and if she confesses and change her heart, it still doesn't nullify the things already set into motion by the sin. Like a bee sting. The stinger has been removed, but the sting remains."

"David, the King of Israel, if you recall, confessed his many transgressions, one of which was the treacherous lie, but he still had to ride the tidal wave in his life from the sins that he committed. Ananias and Sapphira not only held back from giving to the Lord, but they also lied about it to the Holy Spirit, blaspheming Him; this is the one unpardonable sin. The lie is never alone." He stopped to wonder if that last example was appropriate. "Of course," he added, "He struck them dead, but I don't think that will happen here, for Tiffany has not blasphemed the Holy Spirit, she lied to her dad, which is bad enough, but forgivable."

"God knows Tiffany's heart, as he knew the hearts of Ananias and Sapphira. Their hearts were wicked, blackened, hardened and turned; the Truth was no longer in them. It was too late for them; their act was the final straw. Who, except God, knows of the lies and deceit that they had done before God struck them dead for committing the unpardonable sin?"

Victor, hanging his head lower and lower it seemed, clung to his mentor's words, and he whispered a quick prayer in his mind, *Please Lord, I know she has done wrong, but please don't take her. Please let me protect her.* Then he smiled with excitement as an idea came to him. "I can send others to warn her. Maybe Heather, or Mike, or…" he stopped to think if anyone else that could be sent. Not the pastor. He doesn't know of the situation. Victor could only impress upon him to pray for her, and he will. Her parents already pray for her. *Who else can I send?*

One of the Watchers most difficult tricks was to suggest an idea into the mind of another through the power of the Holy Spirit; a way to impress upon the heart of the other believer to help rescue one who had gone astray. The strongest and closest to God are the easiest to reach. It usually took only one or two words, "Help Tiffany," for example.

This action would be impossible without the Holy Spirit. It was only possible with those who have accepted and are still close to God.

Victor had decided. He could still stop the sin that followed a lie, which is often another lie. It was too late to stop the falling of the dominoes that would result from the original sin. He would send a message through the Holy Spirit to Tiffany's pastor, an extra message to her parents and send the message to Heather with two simple words, "Help Tiffany." Heather was very faithful, and he knew she would not hesitate to help once she received the message.

"You good?" Raul asked as he turned to go.

"I guess so. I just need to quit pouting and get to work, right?"

"Right! You pulled my words right from me before I could speak them. Pouting solves nothing. Trust in the Holy Spirit, He will guide you in what to do next." Raul sighed as he left. "I must go. I have a new Angeling, you know. He reminds me a lot of someone I once knew, so troublesome times are ahead." He laughed as he flew away.

"Don't be too hard on him." Victor smiled.

"Oh, I will," his voice echoed from the distance, "it's my job." With that, he left, and shortly after Victor also descended from the cloud.

Chapter Six

Tiffany sat in the lunchroom in the same place she always had and with the same friends that were always there. She didn't eat lunch. She liked nothing they served most of the time, so she didn't even bother. Everything seemed as it had always been. Then, someone who never came and sat at her table before joined the break; Heather. Heather had a different lunch period, and she always sat with her boyfriend.

"May I sit?" Heather asked. *Why is she here?* Tiffany thought. *It's not her lunch period.* Of all the people she wanted to see on that day, Heather was not it. Guilt poured over Tiffany as Heather stood next to the table, holding her tray. Tiffany felt uncomfortable, and she should have. Heather noticed her squirming; who wouldn't have? Tiffany's guilt mentally echoed throughout the room.

"Uh, sure," she replied, shifting in her seat some more. She watched Heather sit down, but couldn't bring herself to look into Heather's eyes. "It's not your lunch period. Why are you here? Is everything okay?"

"Oh, I have a doctor's appointment this afternoon. I'm signing out so I thought I'd grab lunch early, and what better time than when my good friend Tiffany is having lunch?" Her smile was sweet and genuine, as was her aura.

Victor held pride in the way he had gotten Heather and Tiffany together that day. This had been one of his more brilliant works to date. He had impressed upon the doctor's office to change Heather's appointment so that she would have to sign out and take an early lunch. They called her that morning as she headed out of the door. Her mother answered the phone and relayed the message to her as she got into her car. *The Lord works in mysterious ways;* he thought with a smile. *And so do Watcher Angels.*

Although two years apart in school, Heather and Tiffany knew each other very well. Tiffany respected and loved Heather greatly. They went to the same church in the same Sunday school class. They were even on the cheerleading squad together. The thing that they had in common the most, they were open about their relationship with God.

They had known each other since they were young and were almost like sisters. They never had a problem with each other being around. Until that day.

Her good friend, ha. Some friend I am. Tiffany's guilt piled on. *If she only knew what I did. I used her and Mike.* She felt so devious and so trapped. A trap of her own making. *What do I do? What if she asks me about tonight?*

Victor heard and felt the same sensation he had felt before, "LIE!" *No. Not again. No more lies.* Victor doubled his efforts and through the Holy Spirit of the Almighty God, he sent the same message that he had sent earlier to Heather, "Help Tiffany." This communication proved difficult, but is even possible for humans to do this through prayer. If the person did not have the Holy Spirit in them, then it became far more difficult for any Angel to speak with them. Even the high and mighty messenger Angels found much difficulty in getting through. Well, they would just reveal themselves in these instances. Some rules were different for them, dire situations and all. This also had to be done sometimes where Christians are stubborn, or not where they should be in their walk with God.

"Are you okay, Tiff?" Heather had an authentic look of concern on her face. Heather had always referred to her as Tiff, as did Mike and many others in her Sunday school class. They were like family to her, so she and Heather were sisters. So many times they helped each other and had gone through so many things together. Their bond of friendship could never break. A threefold chord. It could not tear, but, at the moment, Tiffany's end was fraying.

Stay calm, Tiffany, you can get through this. "Sure," she replied, giving her best fake smile. "why do you ask?" Tiffany should have realized that this wouldn't work on Heather, for she could read Tiffany like a book. The eyes.

A person not only smiles with their mouths but also with our eyes. When the eyes do not match the smile, then those who are observant, or know us well, will know when that smile is only on the surface. Heather knew everything wasn't quite right, and Tiff had something weighing on her mind. Something BIG. Although she smiled, her eyes showed her pain, even her guilt. Heather noticed.

"Are you sure? I mean, I just felt like you needed to talk or something." Heather had the kindest heart that anyone would ever know, and everyone who knew her didn't know anyone nicer or more genuine than she. Mike, her boyfriend of a long time, much to the chagrin of the ladies, was just as strong. Everyone said that they would probably marry after High School because they were made for each other. But they had plans to wait until after college or for the perfect time, trusting in God. They would know when. They had the love story that many young ladies dreamed of or read about in those Christian romance novels.

Tiffany knew a lot of girls who fawned over Mike. He was like a brother to her. No one else ever caught the eyes of Heather and Mike, except each other. A love that would last a lifetime and more. The way it should be.

Heather placed her fork in the plate and put her hand on Tiffany's arm, bending down to look her in the eye because Tiff's were downcast and avoiding contact with Heather's at all costs. She fiddled with a string of her pants. Heather spoke with love and concern, and Tiffany knew this because she could read it in her eyes. "Well, if you need to talk... I'm here." She gave Tiffany another sweet smile.

"Okay," she replied, only looking up long enough to respond. Her immense guilt kept her from looking into Heather's eyes for too long, so she distracted herself with something on the table beside her. Heather continued to eat.

"Got any plans for tonight?" she said cordially.

Tiffany snapped her eyes up to Heather, who was not looking at her and the guilt in her panged so strong that she could literally hear it in her ears as her heart skipped a beat and a lump formed in the throat. *What do I do? If I tell her, she will try to talk me out of it and then what ...*

The same vibrant PANG echoed through Victor's mind and that one word joined the onslaught, stronger and louder than ever before. "LIE!" *No, not again, they're coming too easy now,* he thought. He gritted his teeth and clamped his eyes shut, not knowing what else to do so he just repeated to himself as if he were trying to put the thought into Tiffany's head, *No lies. No lies. No lies. The truth shall make you free. No lies. NO LIES!* If anyone could have seen Victor at that moment, they would have thought him a lunatic. Well, frantic maybe.

Tiffany's will prevailed, and before Victor could even breathe after his thought, Tiffany tossed the lie out so fast it could have made everyone's head spin. She glanced at Kessie who had just joined them, "Kessie and I are going to the Mall in Savannah tonight, and maybe catch a late-night movie." Kessie whipped her head at Tiffany and then looked at Heather, smiling and nodding her head in affirmation. Tiffany didn't look at Heather.

Disappointment crippled Victor and left him speechless. Thoughtless. Numb. He hated the new rollercoaster that he had been riding and wished to get off before he puked in the seat.

Tiffany couldn't have liked it much, either. She didn't want to lie to her lifelong friend, but felt like she had no choice. If she told the truth, then she would have to explain everything. So, to keep from disappointing Heather, Tiffany lied to her. A rationalization; one spun from a mind clouded by sin.

"Well, at least you guys won't be going to that awful party by the river tonight." Heather spoke with a bit of disgust at the thought of the entire ordeal.

PANG! Tiffany's heart skipped another beat as the guilt

within her ricocheted off the walls of her mind and echoed. *What do I do now?* She was in a state of panic, and Victor was insane with helplessness.

PANG! "LIE!" *STOP IT!* Victor thought, now gripping the side of his skull with both hands. *Stop it, please. You're killing me.*

"Yeah," Tiffany finally responded. "That's just going to be a drunk and drug fest, and God only knows what else. I don't want to be there. Nothing but a bunch of losers and dopers." She still didn't look at Heather and glanced at Kessie, hoping she would confirm her lie and Heather would go away. She hoped the guilt would go with her.

Tiffany loved Heather, but at that moment her presence annoyed Tiffany. If she looked deep into herself, she would find Heather was not the true source of her disdain; it was herself. Heather was just the object that revealed that guilt to her. This was not a fair way to treat her lifelong friend, who only cared about her and wished to help her. In Tiffany's mind, quickly becoming as hardened as her heart, she didn't need or want Heather's help. She just wanted her to leave and take the guilt with her.

Heather stopped eating and put her fork on the tray. "Well, I have to get ready for my doctor's appointment." She stood to go. "Remember, Tiff, if you need to talk, you know where to find me and you have my cell number, you can call or text me anytime."

No, Victor begged, *don't leave. You haven't convinced her of anything or helped her yet.* Then he remembered one of the most sacred truths. People will only remit when and if they choose to remit, quit when they choose to quit, and stop when they choose to stop; no sooner and no later. With a sigh of disappointment, his chin dropped to his chest. *It's going to be a long night.*

Kessie looked over at Tiffany with a wide-eyed expression of surprise and said after Heather left, "Girl, I can't believe you just lied to her." She turned away and smacked her lips while playing with her fingernails. "There may be hope for you yet."

"There may be hope for her yet!" Victor sneered. *Who is influencing whom here?* He knew Tiffany had a lot of influence over

Kessie, because Kessie adored her, looked up to her; almost worshiped her because of her respect for her. Something had gone insanely wrong, a reversal of roles, and to Victor it all stunk of evil and contempt. *Jason*, he thought with a cringe. *Oh, the frightful monsters that one lie can unleash in the hearts of humanity.*

A lie is like Pandora's Box in ancient mythology. Once the box opened, it could never be closed again. All the carnage and chaos that ensued threatened to destroy the world. Victor refused to believe he could not make this right. As long as he was still around, he could find a way or die trying.

Chapter Seven

When Jason walked into the lunchroom, all the guilt of deceit washed away from Tiffany's mind like South Georgia pollen in a downpour of rain. Her lusts boiled within her as she watched. Her heart gave a drum roll when he sat at her table. She flashed a genuine smile, but her eyes revealed something different within her. Something Victor had never seen there before; something carnal.

He didn't like it at all.

A gambit of emotions flushed through Tiffany; she thought she was in love. Victor believed this boy had placed under some sort of enchantment. Something about this guy raised red-flags of caution within Victor, but he just couldn't put his finger on what could incite such a reaction. It was more than mere jealousy, a type that a father has for his daughter.

Victor loved and adored her similarly, but his love for her differed from anything human. It may have been a part of Victor's contempt for this boy, but he knew that what he sensed in the boy went far deeper than petty jealousy. Call it angelic intuition. As a part of his job to watch and protect, he had to be aware and ready for any sort of trouble.

It wasn't *love* that Victor saw in Tiffany's eyes that day. He had seen love in those eyes when she was six years old, and he had carried her to safety after she had fallen from a tree. She showed love to him, that perfect stranger who had rescued her. As he carried and consoled her, her pain and fear seemed to disappear. She showed trust in her helplessness as Victor walked her to safety. I seemed natural.

He connected with those eyes in such a way once before…

when she was but a newborn babe. *I wonder if she remembers that day.* He shook the thought away.

Victor saw love in her eyes many times with her father and mother, but that was a different type of love. When she came to the altar and her pastor led her to Christ, great love rushed through her and it showed in her eyes then: for God and even for her pastor, another man whom she adored and rightly so. Those were different love than a person may hold for the one for whom they pine.

What Victor saw in the eyes of Tiffany was not love, although full of passion, it remained something far different from love. She responded to what she saw on the surface. She had a longing, but no love.

At that moment, Tiffany didn't know the difference. No other boy ever made her heart patter like it did when Jason was around. When she looked at those golden-brown eyes, she became lost in them. She saw nothing deeper because she didn't look into them, only at them. If she tried, she couldn't have gotten past the surface of those eyes. Jason, a handsome exterior with a polite disposition, had nothing except what he allowed others to see. Nobody noticed what lurked deep behind his golden-brown eyes. Those who took a deeper look would find a void cast from deep in the soul, which echoed from the abyss.

Victor saw it, that deep dark secret, hidden by the shell of an alluring presence. Tiffany didn't seem to care about anything beyond the good looks and charm.

She thought she was in love with him, but was in love with the idea of him. That she caught him when no other girl could feed her massive ego. Small, beautiful frame, but an ego the size of Texas.

There he stood, a good looking, tall, well-built spectacle of a young man; a nice guy and mysterious to boot. It didn't seem to bother Tiffany that she knew nothing about this guy, his past, his parents, where he lived, anything. The mystery about him drew her to him, and a part of the alluring spell he seemed to have cast on most of the young girls around him.

As Jason sat across from her, Tiffany had set in her mind to remedy her not knowing anything about him. *If he's truly a great guy, then even a little lie is worth it.* Her eyes bore into him as she thought. He stared back, revealing nothing.

"So, where are you from, Jason?" she asked after her most intense stare.

He appeared a bit set back. He smiled nervously. Tiffany's eyes still cut through him, but playfully.

He shifted in his seat, unprepared for this sudden onslaught. Victor, who had been sulking and thinking of how his precious Tiffany had pulled away, perked up because he liked that Tiffany finally started making a little sense. Maybe she would find out something about him she didn't like and call the whole thing off. Maybe he would avoid her questions and aggravate her enough to toss him aside and move on. This brought a hope that Tiffany may get out of this mess and savor whatever dignity that remained in her before it was too late. *That's my girl,* he thought, *it's about time.*

"Adams," He said with a chuckle, "My last name is Adams, and I am from, well, here and there."

"Here and there?" Her look changed to one of disgust at the vague answer to her second question, "What kind of answer is that?"

Victor welled with pride. *Yeah, that's my girl alright. Get him.* He stared with intimidation, as if Jason could see him. *Yeah; you gave the wrong answer, Bub. Bub?* He mused, *who says Bub? Who am I, Wolverine?* He shook off the last thought and returned his focus to the conversation.

"It's kind of hard to explain," He said, tapping his pencil on the table and watching it bounce, "I'm a… or I was, a military brat. My parents moved around a lot, so I am not really *from* anywhere."

Pah, Victor thought with a laugh, *that's the lamest thing I've ever heard, she'll never buy that.*

"Your parents were in the military?" A rhetorical question.

Here it comes, Victor thought with a smile, *she's going to strike, lower the hammer; let him have it.*

"Yeah," he replied, "well, my dad was in the Army. He's retired now."

Tiffany studied the boy for a moment. Victor felt giddy. *Here it comes. I love it and I can't wait. Let him have it, baby.*

"I think that's so cool." Her interest piqued, "It's awesome that your dad served this country."

Yeah, Victor got caught up in the moment, *that's my g... wait, what!* "Cool?" no. *NO, it's not cool. It's bad; he's lying, has to be.* He had become so flustered that he lost his grammar skills. *Can't you see this guy is bad news? He, he...* Victor lowered his head again. He may *have been honest, and the children of military members are a special breed and should have an honor that is all their own.*

Victor looked at Tiffany's eyes with shock, and he noticed a slight change to the glow in her eyes that resembled love, but closer to admiration. It pained him to see her being lured into a trap. *Maybe this guy isn't so bad after all.* Victor didn't like what he thought; it confused him.

"My parents moved here several weeks ago after my dad retired." Jason said, "He's from here and always wanted to go back home. Fort Stewart is the closest Army base close, and it's an hour away. They did not station him there, although he tried. So, wanting to come home after retiring, here we are." Jason tapped his pencil still; it was getting on Victor's nerves. It could have been the boy that was getting to him, or that Tiffany couldn't see right through him, or even that Victor himself had weakened towards him. He still had his doubts. Red flags, though.

The thing that bothered him the most was that awful feeling that he couldn't shake, the one given to him by his angel's extra sense. Jason was hiding something. Something big.

"Isn't that hard, moving all the time?" She hung her head. "And then your dad having to go overseas to war. That had to be tough. Don't see how you could stand it. I've been in Beckley, Georgia, my entire life and couldn't think about moving anywhere else." She shrugged. "It had to be hard always moving and wondering where you would be next."

"What?" Victor said aloud and looked at her, pointing to the boy. "You're not falling for the old, 'I was a military brat so feel sorry for me' act, are you?"

"Nah," Jason shrugged. "It's not so bad once you get used to it. This is only my second High School and since my dad retired, I'll probably stay here, and I like it here, so why not stay? And besides," he looked up with wanting eyes and changed his voice; "I like the view." She smiled and blushed, never removing her gaze from his.

"What?" Victor couldn't stand it anymore. His mind flailed. Any connection that he may have been having for Jason disappeared. "You little smooth-talking punk, you'd better be glad I'm just a watcher and I'm not allowed to touch you, or I'd… and who do you think you are with those eyebrows flexing and that," he pointed and waved, "that voice, 'I like the view.'" He mocked.

"I'm really looking forward to tonight," Jason said, changing the subject.

"Yeah," she replied, "It should be fun." She sighed, changing her countenance. "But to be honest, I'm not very fond of parties. All the drinking and drugging, it's not my thing, you know. We can always go somewhere else." *Like out with Heather and Mike,* she thought. Guilt clung to her like socks did to jeans without a dryer sheet. She still tried to make things right. *I'll apologize to my parents later,* she thought, *they'll forgive me.*

Victor had found a ray of hope in her last statement and settled down. *We can still salvage this situation. This can be a test for this young man. Maybe he'll be a gentleman and take her somewhere else, like she asks. She could call Heather and they could go out together, then she wouldn't have lied. She…* Victor hoped upon hope, but he knew the law. He knew making a truth out of a lie still meant the lie had to have been told to begin with. It wasn't the words *per se* that were wrong, not alone anyway, but the intent of the heart. *Well, at least she is trying,* he thought.

"Well, you don't have to take part," Jason said. "just come

along for the fun of being there with all of your friends."

Kessie, who had been pretending to carry on a conversation with someone else, all the while listening to them, chimed in, "That's right girl. It wouldn't be the same without you." She reached out and put her arm around Tiffany and hugged her close. "You've got to be there."

"Well, okay," she nodded, "It will be nice to hang out with my friends." She laid her head on Kessie's shoulder, "for you, my boo."

Victor sat, helpless and stunned. *If only she were still six years old, pure and innocent. Why do they have to grow up?* He thought to no one in particular, but knew that God was listening, so he prayed. *Why can't I just appear and talk to her, to make this all stop before it is too late?*

Then he remembered the lesson that he had learned all those years before, and the inquisition that followed his actions. He knew well the rule of non-interference and the consequences of such an action. If he was going to rescue Tiffany, he would have to risk it all. He had always been listening, willing to die for her, and feared that soon he may have the chance. Things spiraled out of control like a category five tornado. Victor longed to return to the time when Tiffany was young, to simpler times.

Chapter Eight

Ten years earlier.

To Victor, it seemed to have all happened yesterday, a breezy spring afternoon, a touch of humidity, and the coolness to the air of early spring, barely a cloud in the sky; the perfect day to play outside. Tiffany, then six years old, loved to play by the creek in the wooded area behind her enormous back yard. She climbed the biggest tree that she could find. It had to be at least a hundred years old. Her favorite tree. The cool shade it provided and the unknown age gave feed to her active imagination. That day she climbed.

"Don't climb that tree," Victor admonished as she continued to climb. "And not so high, you may fall." Victor knew she couldn't hear him, but that never stopped him from trying to warn her. She was always the daring sort.

Victor was as nervous as a gun-shy dog at a cannon shooting contest. He looked around and see if anyone was nearby to come to her aid, if she were to fall. The tree by the creek sat too far away for anyone to hear her scream or see her fall. One drawback of having a big wooded back yard on the outskirts of a small town.

And the local hospital. He shuddered at the thought. She climbed higher and higher while Victor, with little experience at that sort of thing, became more and more nervous the higher that she climbed. Up she went with no fear or regard of danger. "Ok," he called up to the tree, "that's high enough. You can come down now." He didn't care if she couldn't hear him, yet hoped that somehow, she could.

Tiffany embraced every challenge in her life with the same

tenacity. Nothing would stop her from her goals, and nothing would hold her back from doing what she had set in her mind to do. Her stubbornness would get her into a lot of trouble, as it would cause her to succeed where many believed that neither she nor any other could. She finally stopped climbing and Victor breathed a sigh of relief and thought that she would climb back down. Not really. To his surprise, she sat on the nearest limb with her feet dangling below her, swinging. He reached out as if to catch her if she should come down the hard way, and then he remembered he couldn't. It was the most cardinal rule of the Watchers. "Never reveal yourself to the Child of God that we assigned you to watch." It also proved to be the hardest rule to follow. He had been with her with all watchers since the day of her birth, and to stand by and watch... *Torture.*

There Tiffany sat, as beautiful as a six-year-old girl as there ever was, with eyes bright as the sea flowing into the sky. She stared at the sky as the soft clouds rolled slowly by and reflected upon her stare. Then she sang. The tune was very familiar to Victor, and her precious little voice sent chills down his spine. If he hadn't been in love with this little darling before, he surely would become that way soon.

> *Jesus loves me, this I know,*
> *For the Bible tells me so,*
> *Little ones to him belong*
> *They are weak, but he is strong*
> *Yes, Jesus loves me*
> *Yes, Jesus loves me*
> *Yes, Jesus loves me*
> *For the Bible tells me so.*

It may surprise some to learn that angels can cry. When little Tiffany, Victor's darling, sang that song, it not only sent chills down his spine, but it also sent tears streaming down his face. The realization of how lucky a Watcher Angel he had been to have such a wonderful young lady to watch overwhelmed him with joy. Raul told marvelous stories of Jesus from His childhood, and those stories blessed Victor to no end. Raul was His Watcher, the most privileged of all the Watchers in heaven to be afforded such a great honor as to be the Watcher Angel for the One and only begotten Son of the Living God.

Although Tiffany was not the Son of God, she was indeed an angel to him, and Victor always felt blessed for the ability to share in her life. As the song came to a close the second time, a powerful gust of wind knocked her off balance from her limb. With a scream, she fell to the ground; almost thirty feet. With reflexes like lightning, Victor rushed over to her and solidified in the human realm as he ran, but he could only partly appear before she hit the ground. Unable to get there soon enough to catch her, he materialized enough to slow her rapid descent. If she had hit that hardened, root infested ground from that height at full force, it would have killed her in an instant.

After she hit the ground, Victor, who had become completely solid, reached down and scooped the young princess into his arms. It had knocked her unconscious, either from the fall or from the shock of it. Victor didn't care that they could see him; he just knew that he had to care for his little angel. Besides, he would appear to be a young man. No one would know that he was an angel.

As he carried her back to her house on the long walk from the creek through the woods and into the backyard, she opened her eyes. Those piercing blue eyes stared right into the heart of Victor, and when he looked at her, he realized for sure. "It's okay, little doll, you came down from the tree the hard way. You're very fortunate that I was there to pick you up. I'll take you home so that your Mommy can take care of you." She noticed the pain and tears welled up in her eyes. "Shhh," he said, stroking the side of her face with the back of his finger. "Don't worry now. I'm here to help you. Victor will make everything alright. Just relax." She went back to sleep.

It wasn't long before he got to the house, knocked on the door, handed Tiffany over to her mother and explained how he had "*found*" her out by the creek and how he "*thought*" she had fallen from a tree.–Someone would later remind him of this little omission; bending the truth. (Omitting the truth in any circumstance is the same as telling a lie. The intent was to deceive, cover up, or deter one from the truth. No matter how polished, rationalized or necessary it seemed, it was still a lie.)

Later, when Tiffany awoke in the hospital bed, the bruises showed and they had already set her broken arm in a cast. She looked at everyone and appeared a bit confused, like she was looking for someone who was not in the room. "Victor?" She asked, but for the first time in her life, Victor was not there.

"Who is Victor?" Tiffany's father asked.

The mother shrugged and said, "That's probably the name of the boy who picked her up and brought her home."

Victor had not been there to hear her call out his name because they had already summoned him to the council of Angels to explain his actions on that day. The angel authorities were swift to take action and swift to judgment. They had called Victor back to heaven to stand trial for his actions. Someone else for that moment had to watch over Tiffany.

Chapter Nine

At the Council of Angels in Heaven, still 10 years earlier.

Gabriel and Michael sat before him. Michael glared. The middle seat remained empty. A trumpet sounded. Everyone stood as the Christ entered and when He sat down at the judgment seat everyone else took their seats, ending with Victor and his Angelic Council, Raul.

Raul held a place of high esteem amongst the Angels, and he was the most respected of all the Watcher Angels. Being the Watcher of the and only begotten Son of God carried a lot of weight in those parts. The Christ adored him as well, for He had gotten to know him after He returned to His home in glory.

Oh, the stories they could reminisce. Often a gathering would grow when they talked of old times. Nothing of recorded history existed of the childhood of Jesus Christ, so that made it extra special as the only two who knew all the greatest details were Jesus and Raul. They even knew a lot of things that Jesus' mother Mary didn't know, and it surprised her to hear some stories.

It may come as a surprise, but Jesus, completely human while on the earth, acted no differently than any other child. He had the Spirit of God within Him, with all the wisdom that goes with being God, but as for being a human child, He was just like the rest, human. Jesus felt pain, bled, suffered loss, and even had some down days. He endured temptation, but chose not to sin.

Jesus and Raul became the closest of friends. Although Christ loves everyone equally, He had an extra special place in his heart for Raul. No one, except the Almighty Father, knew Jesus

Christ better. Of course, Raul told many of those stories from Jesus' youth to who he trained so they took part in that life as well.

"Will the accused please rise?" Michael's voice halted the memory and Victor returned to reality to see the stern face of Michael staring. *Accused,* Victor thought as he stood in a slow, awkward motion, Raul stood with him. "Victor, Watcher Angel third class," (the lowest rank for a Watcher Angel) "you stand accused of breaking the Angelic Code by revealing yourself to a human being without gaining permission to do so and for bending the truth in the attempt to hide your true identity."

"The first," Gabriel spoke up, his voice much more repose than Michael's, "is a violation against the Angelic Code and the second not only violates our Code but also breaks the laws of humankind. A lie is one of the deadliest of all sins, and bending the truth is a lie." He paused for effect. "A half-truth is still a whole lie. A touch of truth camouflages it and could be even more damaging. Omission of the truth is a lie."

The Angelic Council always convened at the Judgment Seat of Christ for any infraction against the Angelic Code or the laws of humanity. Christ often used the seat after the death of humans, but only on rare occasions was it used for an Angel. The council comprised three: God the Son Jesus Christ along with Michael and Gabriel, heaven's archangels - the supreme commanders of all the angels in heaven and upon the earth. They would hear and see all the evidence presented and then pass judgment upon the accused.

This differed from the Judgment with the humans, because what they saw would be their life in retrospect, where they could have done more, what they had done well since salvation and what reward that they had earned or lost through their lives as Christians. And humans sat in the seat alone, their only council being Jesus Christ, who also held the role as their judge.

One could only describe the hall that housed the Judgment Seat as magnificent. Its walls and floors held a glossy, almost silvery/blue, but not completely transparent type of glass. Christ sat in the middle seat, the Judgment Seat, and Michael and Gabriel occupied the two seats next to Christ.

The room itself, beyond the Judgment Seat platform, seemed quite small; a small desk, big enough for two, the accused and his counsel, and two seats for them to sit. Angels chose counsel to present alternate views, or reasons for the infraction against the Code. Calm luminescence emitted from everything deep within the surroundings as to not blind or flash, yet it was enough to keep the room illuminated. It gave everything an iridescent glow.

As the trial began, the five found themselves inside a scene from Victor's mind. The walls became some sort of hollow matrix and all parties stood within the midst of a memory.

In the surrounding scene, everyone could see Tiffany, but not Victor. The memory was Victors, shown from his point of view. At that point of the memory, he still presented within the spiritual realm. Victor's eyes wetted when he heard Tiffany singing about how Jesus loved her. Christ smiled when he saw this as well, for how he loved the little children and found quite a blessing Himself in that song. *It is so true*; He thought.

Then, in the memory, wind blew and knocked Tiffany off balance. Victor winced and turned away, as he didn't want to relive the memory. Then, in the memory, he rushed toward her and when her compact frame almost struck the ground. He had to restrain himself from rushing toward her in reality from within the chamber. Raul noticed him flinch and placed his arm in front of him to steady Victor's natural response.

In the memory, he had gotten to Tiffany just in time and had become just solid enough to slow her descent so that she wouldn't hit the ground with the full force of gravity from the thirty-foot drop. Everyone standing amid the memory from the chamber could see the arms of Victor, which were only partially solidified in the memory.

"Stop!" Michael snapped, and the memory stopped, leaving a still scene around them in perfect resolution. He walked over to the paused image and pointed to the partially revealed arms of

Victor. "What were you doing here, Victor?"

"I was trying to catch her." He said with sarcasm in his voice, which brought a slight smile and a nudge from Raul.

"How do you know it wasn't her time? Do you know for sure that the accident would have killed her?" Michael inquired further.

"I…" Victor pondered. "I didn't know if it was her time or not and hoped it wasn't. As for her accident, a fall of about thirty feet … I think it would have killed her, yes."

Michael pressed on. "You didn't know, so what right did you have to save her? You are not God. Only God knows when the time comes."

"Well," Victor still held a sarcastic tone, "If God *was* ready for her and it was her time, then no matter what I did, I couldn't have stopped it."

Michael cleared his throat, showing his offense to Victor's tone. A touch of Victor's shoulder from Raul told Victor that he needed to be careful in his tone.

"Lord," Raul interjected. Jesus, who had his hands folded in front of Him and two fingers on His lips, responded with a motion of his hand to Raul, signaling for him to continue, "Was it the young lady's time?"

Jesus wagged his head from one side to the other and then resumed his former pose. Raul thanked Him. Michael heaved a sigh.

"You risked exposure," Michael returned to the almost solid image of Victor's arms. "Continue the memory." The memory showed Victor becoming completely solid and his arms were in plain view of everyone when he reached down to scoop the little girl up in them and as he had walked away, holding her tightly to his chest. He looked down and saw one of his feet as it stepped everyone could see the girl in his arms. "Stop!" The image froze. "Right there," he said pointing, "what if someone saw you carrying the girl?"

"You don't think I should have left her there all alone when I could help her, do you?" Victor responded. His voice again held a disgusted tone. "And if someone would have seen me, as it was, or will be in this memory, with her mother, they would have seen me as a young boy. I did not arraign myself in angelic glory."

"We Angels are not to be seen by humans except for only special occasions and great emergencies." He pointed at the little girl again. "All she had was a few scrapes and bruises and a broken arm. You slowed her enough to save her. You should have left her there. Someone would have found her."

"Someone would have found her?!" Victor's voice grew more intense. Raul reached out to calm him again. "Really?" Victor continued after calming himself. "Just how long do you suppose I should have waited? An hour, a day… weeks. I saw that my little girl needed help, and I acted according to instinct and my training. Maybe because you have had negligible contact with them, you cannot understand the gravity, pun intended, of this situation and you don't understand humans. They need a lot of help, encouragement even. If she would have woken up alone, she would have been sore afraid. Besides, I made sure that they did not see me in my full angelic glory." Raul put his hand on Victor's arm while giving him a look of warning and then a reassuring nod.

"Made sure they did not see you, huh? Skip forward to the house." The memory showed a door opening in front of Victor and Tiffany's mother, looking at him in complete shock. "Stop!" Michael said. "Look at the face of that woman, she looks like she had just seen a ghost, and since they don't exist, it must have been a spirit, or an angel, perhaps."

Raul again appealed to Christ. "She was not shocked because of the appearance of Victor at her door, who I again remind you would have only appeared as a human boy. We all know that when we become solid, we can take on human form when we wish to. We only show our angelic form in extreme circumstances, and that is only when we are battling demons. The mother was shocked, yes, but not from seeing Victor, but because of the battered child in his arms. It is the same reaction that any mother would have given. Lord, I recall your mother having a similar look of shock upon her face when you hanged upon the cross." Jesus nodded in response.

"She knew his name," Michael continued, presenting his case without pause. This shocked Victor and Raul, they looked at each other; Victor just shrugged. "Fresh memory," he called out as a memory foreign to everyone, but Jesus and Michael came into view. "This is from the hospital that cared for Tiffany. It is the memory from one nurse in the room. Unfortunately, after her shift, while on her way home from work, she got killed in a tragic accident. Such terrible things often happen in life." His voice had a solemn tone. He paused for a moment to honor the dead as the silence flowed into the unknown scene. *I'll give this to Michael. He sure is thorough.*

The scene that played before them showed Tiffany waking up in her hospital bed for the first time since Victor brought her home. She opened her eyes, looked around and said one word, a question, "Victor?"

"Stop." The image paused in perfect stillness and in three dimensions. "How does she know your name?"

A single tear rolled from Victor's eye. "Because I told it to her," he admitted, hanging his head. "She was afraid, and I was only trying to ease her fear and her pain."

"Afraid?! Afraid of what? Afraid of whom? You?" Michael said as he was waving to call up the next memory.

"No sir, not of me," Victor replied with confidence. "just afraid. That was only the second time in her life I saw her fear and I couldn't stand to see it in her eyes again." Victor wasn't holding to the memory at hand, but when she was a baby.

The new scene around them Michael called for came from when Victor carried the child to the house to give to her mother, and she looked up at him. Victor got choked up again by her fabulous, deep blue eyes. They could cut through even the hardest of hearts. When the scene got to where he said, "Victor will make everything alright," Michael yelled for the memory to stop. Michael paused in a dramatic silence to let everything soak in before continuing.

"Victor will make everything alright,'" he repeated. "Why did you say that? You told her your name. Why didn't you just say, 'Everything will be alright?'"

"Because she was afraid, and I knew it would calm her." Victor's head was again hanging down.

"Have you said this to her before." He asked.

Victor leaned to speak to Raul before he answered. Raul nodded and Vicor said, "Yes, once before."

"When?"

You mean you didn't know, Victor thought, but wisely kept to himself.

Raul stood and said to no one in particular, "Call into view the first memory from Victor's mind of Tiffany, about a year after he went to earth." They always sent first time Watcher Angels to earth about a year before their assignment's birth. They must get acquainted with the world of humanity and to observe the family of the one they watched.

Before them, a tiny baby lay in an incubator. She had tubes all in her and an IV in her forehead because the nurses couldn't find any veins big enough to get even the smallest needle in anywhere else. Machines flashed and beeped all around her when she opened her big ice-blue eyes. Everyone could tell that she was afraid. She was a small child, born too early, in an enormous world. "Stop," Raul commanded. "Who is this, Victor?"

Victor answered, as another tear streamed from his eye. The fear that in those tiny eyes struck the hearts of them all, "It's Tiffany about a week after she was born."

Raul looked around, and he saw Gabriel wiping a tear from his eye, as did Jesus. Michael attempted a stern pose, but it proved difficult for him as he saw the intense fear on the face of that tiny child. "And, where were you?"

Victor pointed to a certain spot where all anyone could see was a small blur off to the side and he said, "I was right there. We were in a Hospital Neonatal Intensive care unit."

"Continue," Raul ordered. As the scene continued, a hand came into view and the little child grasped.

Another hand came into view and gently rested on the side of the baby's head. "Don't worry now," Victor's voice echoed in the hall. "I'm here to help you. Victor will make everything alright."

Michael wanted to argue, but Raul had not yet stopped the video. When he said stop, the big wonderful blue eyes of the little child were in plain view and they were no longer riddled with fear. They showed a child at complete peace. Even Michael shed a tear from the shock and the beauty of the scene.

Raul continued, "Victor felt little choice but to reveal himself on this occasion, and he had no choice on the other. He made a decision that would help her for a long time. He removed the one thing that destroys more humans than any other emotion. Fear." He looked around before continuing. "Fear is the weapon Satan too often uses to bring God's children to his mercy, make them doubt, and to pull them away."

"All Victor did through a heart of love was battle fear for her when she could not do so on her own. Those few words, 'Victor will make everything alright' did indeed make everything alright, and would continue to do so. In your Word, Lord, you remind humanity repeatedly that there is no reason to fear. Now, how can we fault anyone for acting to remove the one thing that can so easily destroy? When any action drives a spike through one of Satan's greatest weapons, fear, it is always a victory for the good guys."

Michael stood humbled for the first time since the proceedings began. "Well, I now see this angel had little choice in the actions, but it still should come to a vote of the council. There is still the matter of the untruth. Before we get to the other, how does the panel vote on the count of Watcher Angel Victor being revealed to humans?"

"Not guilty," Gabriel said.

"Not guilty," Jesus said and then added, "What he did was unavoidable."

"Not guilty," Michael voted, then continued, "Now as to the other charge..."

"Lord," Victor spoke up, interrupting, "I am guilty of hiding the truth from Tiffany's mother in protecting myself. I intended to deceive and, if asked, would have lied. In fact, I told a half-truth about this. I confess to You and You alone as humanity's judge, and ask for Your forgiveness and mercy for my crimes against humanity. I will suffer whatever repercussion that my actions have put into motion when the time comes."

"Very well," Jesus said as he stood to go, "let that be your punishment." Before he exited, he turned to add, "Never stop loving her, Victor, and know this. I remitted the eternal penalty for your transgression, but the earthy impact is great as the lie is deadliest of all sins. It will happen in her life, and will hurt you to the core when it does. Your actions have already set the repercussions in motion into motion and when it comes, you will know it and will be helpless to stop it. I will not stop it either. Although I have forgiven you and have transmuted the ultimate penalty, the natural chain of events will persist." They all stood as Jesus left, and then Victor turned to Raul, thanking him for his help.

Michael and Gabriel left the chamber, but before Victor returned to the earth, Gabriel called him aside. Although Victor did not receive a charge with the insurgence, Gabriel gave him quite a lecture on how he could have avoided everything and what Victor's actions could have done to all that they held sacred. After his scolding, Gabriel lovingly reminded Victor of his duty to Tiffany and to the rest of the Watchers on the earth. Hanging his head, Victor went back to earth.

Chapter Ten

Some say that the truth hurts. Well, a lie hurts a lot worse, especially when it comes from someone that you love. Victor felt dumbfounded when he saw how the lies came pouring out of the innocent mouth of his dear Tiffany. And with each lie that she told, she darkened her precious soul more. The more lies that are told, the easier it becomes. Victor longed to stop her, to find some way to show her the error before it was too late, but there was nothing he could do. She was a lamb caught in the thicket and Satan, the wolf, was moving in for the kill. Victor thought of nothing to stop the things her choices had set into motion. For the first time since he wound up flat on his face making a run at Raul, he felt powerless.

He understood what Jesus meant about how it would hurt him when the penance for his one failure came to call. Now that day had come. Victor wished that he would have let the Archangel Michael punish him for his crime against humanity instead. The penalty set in motion may be too much for him to bear. He couldn't imagine anything worse than watching his darling Tiffany go astray. Lies were the instrument that Satan, the father of lies, used to lure her away.

It wasn't the lie alone that caused young Tiffany to fail; the tempters also used a handsome young man named Jason. But, the awful lie put her on the slippery slope that would bring her down unless she could find something to grab to hold or Victor could find something to get her off of that slippery slope. But if she didn't notice the slide…

As Victor watched her in the lunchroom, he felt as if everything about her had changed.

***

The bell rang, signaling that lunch period had ended, and the students were to go to the next block of classes. "Pick you up at six thirty?" Jason asked, as they walked out.

"Better make it six," she replied. "My dad wants to meet you."

"Okay, six it is then." He went to his next class. Tiffany watched him for a bit and then turned with a bounce of joy and went on to her class, smiling the entire time.

Victor was so preoccupied that he missed a clue that would have helped him end all this early and would have given him cause to act. As Jason walked away, the slightest moment in the glass's reflection showed a sneer on the face of Jason and if one looked close enough, they could see fire, lust and mischief in his eyes. Something sinister had revealed itself, if even for a moment. For an instant the evil that lived inside of Jason had revealed itself, and no one noticed. The moment passed so quickly that only the trained eye could have seen it. If Victor would have noticed, it would have assured that his suspicions had been true all along. Jason may not be who he portrayed himself to be.

Later, when she got home from school, Tiffany still floated amidst the clouds. She smiled and hummed a popular tune while she got ready, put on her makeup with a smile. When she went into the living room to sit and wait for Jason, the smile remained. At six, the doorbell rang. He was right on time. *Gosh,* she mused, *this guy's doing everything right.* When Tiffany opened the door, she noticed he had flowers in his hand. "For me?" Her ever-present smile broadened.

"No," he nodded, looking around her. "Sorry," he said, then turned his attention to her to give a smooth reply. "They're for the lady of the house."

Brown-nosing punk, what does he think this will do... Victor wasn't able to finish his thought because of Tiffany's mother's overreaction to the unexpected gift from Jason. She even showed them to her husband, who didn't change his expression and just harrumphed in response.

"Aren't they beautiful," she said, elated and then continued as she walked off, "well, isn't he sweet?" She winked at Tiffany as if to say, "Good job," and went into the kitchen to put the flowers in a vase.

"Yeah, yeah, I see them," Tiffany's dad said. "Pretty, yeah." He glared at Jason out of the corner of his eye. *What's this kid up to? He* thought. Naturally he didn't trust any boy that age, and he knew about every trick that existed to get a girl into a compromising position, or at least he thought he did. This was a new one on him. He couldn't help but to admire the gesture. *Giving the mom flowers. Why didn't I ever think of that?* Then he thought a little deeper. *Wait a minute. He didn't bring me anything.* He got up and shook Jason's hand. "Jason," he gave his best gruff voice and stern look, coupled with a tight grip. Nodding, he sat down to return his attention to the television program that he acted like he watched.

Jason, like most of the other boys Tiffany brought home to meet her parents, sat in the chair closest to the door. They must have thought it would have made for a quick escape, just in case. That or they were afraid to go any further into the house.

Tiffany sat with her hands folded between her knees. Nervous. Her dad ignored the boy across the room and stared at the television, watching the news. Or at least acting like it. The truth: he hadn't seen or heard a thing on the TV that because his mind occupied itself with trying to figure out what this smooth joker was up to. *What's his game? He* thought. *Never mind. Dumb question. I know his game.* He gave a quick sideways glance at the boy and returned his attention to the news.

Jason was a cool character, though. More so than any boy his age Tiffany's father had ever known. *Too cool.* He thought as he stared through the TV and contemplated what his next move should be. It seemed as if nothing fazed him, not even the silent treatment, which was his greatest tactic of intimidation.

He stared at the news, ignoring whoever sat in the chair closest to the door. *At least he sat in the chicken chair,* he thought. *As cool as this cat is,* he thought while nodding in his mind, reveling in the minor victory. *He still sat in the chicken chair.* The silent treatment didn't seem to work, and that bothered dad to no end. Jason quietly watched the news with him, waiting for Tiffany's dad to make the next move. Tiffany looked from one and then to the other as she watched this mental tennis match. Her nerves were on edge. Back and forth she looked, wide eyed with apprehension and anticipation. She did this so much that her neck got sore. It seemed like forever before a commercial came on, and her dad muted the TV. Her dad turned his attention to Jason. "What grade are you in, Jackson?" Saying the wrong name; another tactic to instill fear and dominance.

"Eleventh, sir... and it's Jason."

Sir!? This shocked Tiffany. *And without prompts! This guy is good. She thought.*

Sir, her dad thought, *so he passed the first test.* He was still skeptical of the boy, as he would be of any young man Tiffany brought home, especially one that he didn't know. *This guy's too good; too calm. Slick. He's got to be hiding something.* "You, uh, have a job or do you mooch off your parents?"

"Daddy?!" Tiffany scowled at her father.

"What?!" he looked back at her in fake surprise. "That's a good question. I mean, he is taking you out, and it speaks to his quality." She still scowled at him as only a teenage daughter could. He returned his attention to Jason. "Do you work?"

"Haven't found a job yet, sir. We haven't been in this town long, but I have a few coals in the fire." Jason was as cool as a fresh salad.

Coals in the fire, huh? What coals? Drugs? Gangs? Illegal arms trafficking? He stared at Jason while thinking of what to ask next, and Jason returned his gaze without flinching or seeming to give any regard to the mistrust that he knew Tiffany's father was giving him. Tiffany smiled as she looked at the two of them; Jason impressed her, indeed.

"Who is your dad?" Tiffany's dad asked, but before Jason could answer he held up a finger, telling him to wait. He pressed the mute button on the remote because the news was back on. Jason waited for the next commercial before giving an answer.

Everybody fails that test, her dad thought, *but this guy is good.* When the news came back on and Tiffany's dad turned the sound back up, most boys would start answering his last question and ignore the fact that he had turned the sound back on and had returned his attention to the news. Then as they would rattle on, her dad would look at them with a dull expression and point to the television set as if to say, "Shut up! I'm watching the news." Since Jason was the first one to pass this test, Tiffany's dad still didn't hear any of the news before the next commercial break. He could only think about the smoothness of this kid and clamored for a way to trip him up. It never entered his mind that this guy might just be a nice guy. Any guy that wanted to date his daughter, especially on a first date, was a bad guy.

After he saw Tiffany's dad press the mute button, Jason answered the question. "My dad is Colonel Charles Adams, US Army retired. He just retired a few months ago." Jason had put emphasis on the name, "Charles Adams", because he knew that Tiffany's father would recognize the name.

Then something that neither Tiffany nor anyone else in the house expected, ever seen in that situation, happened. Even Victor, who up to this point enjoyed the show and, of course, remained as skeptical as Tiffany's father, became flabbergasted, even speechless, by what transpired next. Tiffany's dad smiled and perked up, turning all of his attention to Jason while turning the television off. At first Tiffany thought that her dad had gotten up to pummel Jason for no reason when he stood but he said, "Charles Adams," with a bit of an excitement in his voice, "Sapling County High School, class of 1992, quarterback of the football team that took us to state during his senior year... *that* Charles Adams?"

Jason mustered a smile. He looked up at the towering figure that now stood almost next to him. "Yes sir, the same."

"Wow," he shook his head, "Chuck Adams," he reached out to grab Jason's hand and Jason stood to shake it, "my daughter is going out with the son of Chuck Adams." He shook Jason's hand vigorously and continued as he let go. "So, how is your dad? Man,

I haven't seen him in twenty years." He looked at Tiffany, whose mouth stood agape in shock, not knowing what to think.

"This guy's dad," he pointed at Jason with one hand while his other rested upon his back, "was the best quarterback this town has ever had. Heck, he was the best athlete this county has ever seen. His picture and trophies are all over the place at the High School. Man, he was everybody's hero. He left to go to some A and M school on a scholarship out west somewhere, Texas, maybe? Over time, everyone lost track of him." He looked at Jason again, the smile fixed to his face. Tiffany sat speechless and shocked. "Joined the Army, eh? And made *Colonel*." Yeah, we all knew he would be something great."

Jason, finally at a loss, just stood there in the silence, watching Tiffany's dad shake his head and stare as if he were remembering the good old days. Then he snapped out of it, "Oh," he said looking at the clock, "wow, it's getting late. You guys should go if you want to make the movie in time." Then, with his next gesture, Tiffany thought she might faint. He pulled out his wallet and handed some money to Jason. "Here," he said, "Since you don't have a job yet, this will allow you to show my girl a good time. You can pay me back later." At first Jason refused it but took it after her dad insisted. Dad reached out, hugged Tiffany, kissing her goodbye, and as he slapped Jason on the back. The two youngsters headed out of the door. They were off to enjoy a delightful meal and a late movie. At least that is what everyone thought. As they walked out of the door, Tiffany heard her dad say, "Chuck Adams' son. He's got to be a good kid." The door closed behind them.

Victor stared in complete shock. He could not believe what he saw. "What are you doing?" Victor screamed. "I can't believe you bought into all of that. Can't you see that this kid is bad news? Am I the only one who thinks he's hiding something behind that pretty boy and good guy facade? Hasn't anyone ever heard the phrase, 'too good to be true'?" Victor was almost insane with fury and helplessness. "If he's such a good kid, why didn't he tell your daughter to tell the truth? Huh? Tell me that."

He didn't care that they couldn't hear him, but so wished that they could.

He stood right in front of Tiffany's father's face, which remained plastered with an odd smile and a far-off gaze. "Why didn't he take her to the movies like she asked him to instead of that party? But, NO, you don't know about that... Hey everybody, meet Tiffany's dad, the next nominee for bonehead father of the year."

Victor continued to rant unheard and unnoticed as Tiffany's dad walked into the kitchen. He followed with haste. "You didn't even ask where Heather and Mike were or if they were going to meet them or anything." He looked at the door. "You didn't even get halfway through with your normal harassment bit that you enjoy so much. Then you just let them leave?" Victor was right next to him again. "Just like that. So that's how it works, huh?" He then changed his voice to continue mockingly, "'Chuck Adams' son. He's got to be a good kid.' Pah."

Victor stormed through the door, literally through the door, and watched after Tiffany. *Tonight*, he thought, *she is going to need me more than she ever has before, I'm afraid.* By the time his rampage ended and he had made it outside, Victor could have kicked himself for his own foolishness. Tiffany and Jason already left. He tried to go to her as he would have any other time through his sense of her presence, but he couldn't. He couldn't feel her presence at all. It was as if she left the planet. For the first time in Tiffany's life, Victor did not know where to find Tiffany. He knew that something had to be amiss because no matter what, he should always be able to find her. *Unless...* He thought as he stood helpless for a moment in the front yard, looking one way down the road and then the other, trying to figure out in which direction they had gone. His heart dropped as he realized what had happened. He lost Tiffany.

Chapter Eleven

(Understanding Angels–lesson 2)

Angels have an extra sense that no human can truly understand. They can sense when other angels are around, even if they can't see them. Watchers could also sense the human that they protected and find them anywhere in the world. This sense was how Victor knew that the other children in Tiffany's family also had Watcher Angels. Millions of angels occupy the earth; most of them Watcher Angels and a few Messenger Angels. Although these Messengers carry no more revelation or prophecy for humanity, which all had long since recorded in scripture, there were certain things that they still do for the Kingdom of Heaven.

Once in a while, one of the big guys, the Archangels Michael or Gabriel, would visit the world, but that hasn't happened for quite a long time. They only came to do a job that no one else could do. Since Michael and Gabriel came with the messages for the first advent of Christ and other than the revelation to John on the Isle of Patmos, there have been no prophecies. Gabriel hasn't been here since the first advent of Christ. (The first advent of Christ arrived through his birth, life, death, burial and resurrection. The second advent, or coming to earth–in this case returning–is yet to come.)

From time-to-time worker angels would visit because humanity and their plot through life fascinated angels. Deep inside, all angels wish to be Watcher Angels, but only a select group receives such a post.

Then there are the demons. Millions of them live on the earth as well. Human beings can't see them either, unless the demon or any of the angels were to reveal themselves. Demons are not privy to the same code as the heavenly angels and don't care, so they have revealed themselves often.

Any time a person thinks that they have seen a ghost, or an apparition, their deceased son, daughter, father, etcetera, or even have thought to have spoken to them, they have encountered a demon and have become prey to their tricks. Demons thrive on fear and superstition; they love to see human beings suffer and love to use their fallacies against them. And they love to tempt and toy with humans, even for entertainment. Especially for entertainment. As fascinated as they are with humanity, demons hate them to the core of their being and no one hates them more than the king of the demons himself, Satan.

To demons, humans were the reason they, then angels and now imps, got tossed from heaven to begin with. Demons, as with Satan himself, their king and the father of lies, are angels, just like Michael, Gabriel, Raul and Victor. Not only are they angels, but they also keep the same powers and their numbers are great.

One-third of the original angels, an unimaginable number to be sure, are now demons. One can only imagine. They outnumber the angels and watchers that are stationed on the earth. If all the watchers and few messenger angels were to give a united front against all the demons, then they would have to fight at least twice as hard and hold them off until reinforcements from heaven arrived. Now, of course in heaven, the number curve changes drastically.

This number differential also plays havoc in trying to watch over God's children, because often those children have many tormentors and the watchers would have to battle them all.

An old cartoon that showed a man with an angel on one shoulder whispering in his ear and a demon on the other shoulder doing the same. This did not show an exact description of true actuality of things. It would have been more accurate to show one angel on one side and a group of demons on the other. The battle for each soul wages each day of the lives of every human being on the earth. And for those who have followed God, just because they have made that choice doesn't mean that the battle is over. They remain on the battlefield and must fight the forces of evil until the day they go home. Hence the need for their watchers.

As for the end, they know who wins the war. None of the angels on the earth worried about losing the war because of being outnumbered; that wasn't their problem.

The problems lay in all the skirmishes between the angels and demons before the end. None of these battles were in the prophecies. No one knew the outcome of them and since the demons were just as powerful as the angels and outnumbered them at least three-to-one on the earth, things rarely bode well for Watcher Angels like Victor if things should take a turn for the worst. Now, the Watchers on the earth, Victor included, always have one distinct advantage over the demons.

God.

***

It's a good thing that my master, Raul, trained me well in the art of fighting demons. He stared into nothingness surrounding the home of Tiffany's family, clamoring for some clue where he may find Tiffany. *I'm afraid I'm going to need those skills before this night is through.*

As mentioned earlier, Victor saw something odd in Jason, but couldn't quite pinpoint what that was. He didn't realize what kept him from noticing what Jason's game may have been until it was too late, but he realized in retrospect, so clearly, that he would have to scold himself because he should have noticed. He didn't have time to kick himself right then, but when he had time, he would do so as hard as he could.

Jason may have fooled Tiffany, her mother, her father, and everyone else, but he hadn't fooled Victor. Victor always knew something didn't quite add up about Jason and reasons he didn't like that kid kept brewing within his mind. He just couldn't nail it down until he saw what he saw in Tiffany's living room moments before the two left. The fullness of this truth didn't come to him until after Jason and Tiffany left. When one sees things in retrospect, they see them more clearly and notice little anomalies that had always been there but failed to see before? This is how Victor's memory clued him in.

Victor had referred to Jason as a kid, but he now realized that Jason was not a kid at all but a demon and, in his hindsight, Victor could see it all clearly.

There is a way to mask the sense of another angel's presence. Why? Only to deceive. It is a tough skill to learn, but possible. An angel can hide from a human forever because, but to hide from another angel is close to impossible. To mask the sense took great concentration. Lose hold of that for even a moment, and the trick reveals itself.

When Tiffany's dad took Jason by surprise when approaching him earlier, Jason lost his hold for just a moment and for that moment Victor could sense him. It was but a flicker of a sense and Victor foolishly let pass as an anomaly, a glitch in the spiritual realm, so to speak. Maybe a simple passing of another angel close by. But in retrospect, he saw things differently. He also knew that Jason could sense his presence and that he had been sensing him all along.

Jason knew Tiffany had a Watcher Angel with her, and that is why he had been so careful in his actions. He had set his trap with great precision and patience, using Victor's clouded judgment and his need to protect Tiffany to sneak right in under his nose.

Now can I kick myself? Not yet. No time.

***

Jason, a demon disguised as a human teenager, had set a trap for the naïve young Tiffany and right now he had her snared in his trap and no one, not even Victor, could come to her aid. He used charm, good looks, and became the perfect suitor in every way; one that every girl would want to say was theirs and would be proud to bring home to meet her parents. It was too good to be true because deep below that robust exterior beat the heart of a demon, a ghoul, the vilest creature in all of creation, and there he sat in his stolen car, driving Tiffany to only God knows where. Tiffany sat right beside him, still unaware of her imminent danger, and the true identity of the one she saw as and believed to be the perfect boy. A disguise donned by a conniving villain. A role well played.

———

The same trick that the demon had used to mask his sense from Victor would now hide Tiffany. Her deception also blocked the Spirit from her. Victor felt helpless and blind, but he would not let that stop him. He had to find Tiffany, and he had to save her before it was too late. Fortunately, he knew exactly where to look, the party at the river. And the worst part of it all, time ran short. Midnight approached quickly, and now Victor knew what Jason had planned to do.

***

(Understanding Angels–Lesson 3)
In heaven, time does not exist. It's not that time stops, fades away, speeds up, it never existed there. One of the most difficult elements of the training for watcher angels had to endure were lessons on time. The first lesson in the class started with defining time. The concept was foreign to them.

Things on earth begin and end, but for a Heavenly Creature, although there is a beginning of sorts, they have had nothing to compare an ending to. Even if they get killed, a new existence begins. This is like the eternal life of human beings, but they must first see death. For an angel, this is but a transformation.

The same God that created humanity created angels, so there must be some similarities. Each of them was first created, kind of like a birthday, and given a task in life. As for an end... death... ceasing to exist, an angel never has to face such things, so the concept eluded them. Hence the need for it in the training and the complication thereof.

God created time for humanity when they fell from grace in the Garden of Eden. Hs grace would not force them to live in an imperfect world forever with imperfect bodies. The angels, however, except for those of the fallen third, do not completely understand the curse of death. Or, time.

Heaven assigned all Watchers who completed the training for someone to watch over and, without delay, sent them to earth. Imagine how strenuous life would be if they came to the human realm with no concept of the ticking clock, endings of any sort, or even the setting sun.

Much of the training at the Watcher Academy was one on one between the mentor and the trainee; in Victor's case, he spent most of his training period with his mentor, Raul. There were certain lessons, though, that the mentor/trainers taught as a group. Many academic subjects that the watchers had to learn fit into these categories and one of the most dreaded classes in the academy was the *Concepts of Time* class. Professor Einstein was the latest instructor of the class, but there had been many through the years that were the instructors. These were always those humans with aptitudes inclining toward time and math and an inhuman understanding of time and space. God gifted them this way for just such a purpose.

Everything about the class confused the young Watchers to be. Taught near the completion of the training, the course held a place of dread for them from the beginning. The concept of how things end was the second lesson that Einstein taught.

He always began his lessons with the same phrase, "Time ends, and thus this class on time ends, as does your training at the end of this class." He would proceed with painstaking mental lessons on time and space, death, and endings. Every student's mind would spin so fast with confusion that some of them would become dizzy and faint. Over *time*, as they learned it to be, they would grow to look at the heaven that they had always known in a different light.

After being confused for a significant period and trying to grasp a foreign concept, the angels would get to the concept of the final exam. As Einstein had told them at the beginning of their lessons in time, if they finished the course, at its end, their training would also end. They would graduate, but no one could graduate unless they passed the course on time. Those who could not pass the final exam had to take the class of time, time and time again until they passed it or washed out.

After passing the class and proceeding to the graduation, the trainees would joke about how the class seemed to last forever. The newer students in the academy never got the joke until it came to the *time* when they also had to take the class, although they always laughed as if they did.

The final exam proved the most arduous task of all. If after repeated tries and one could not pass the test, then they would become a worker angel and they would never allow them to go to the earth for more than brief visits or vacations.

The worst part of the final exam for the class was that it had a time limit. If someone got that irrevocable part of the test wrong, or ran out of time, then they would. In learning the concept of time, one must not act as if they had all the time in the world. The greatest lesson on time rested in the knowing that it always ends.

***

When Victor began his search for Tiffany, he knew he was in the largest race against time that he had ever faced. He knew that if he didn't find her soon, he would have to go back to heaven and face his mentor Raul, among the others, as a failure. These things paled compared to his greatest worry.

He didn't want to lose Tiffany; he could not imagine life without her. Sure, he would get a reassignment and he would grow to love his new assignment, but nobody would ever replace Tiffany in his heart. He had to find her before it was too late; before her life was at an end.

He wanted to think the word *"cloud"* and summon Raul to meet him at any cloud in the air, but he had already delayed too much to even ask his old mentor for advice on this problem, although he could use a pep talk and some wisdom on what to do. If he could only freeze the world at that moment, if even just for a few minutes, and search for her until he found her.

Only Father, if even through an agent, can halt the ticking clock.

God honors the free will of man and their choices above all

things. If they did wrong, then they must also face the consequences of that wrong. *I wish I could go back in time for just a few days,* Victor thought again. Victor had to find Tiffany the hard way, the "human" way, by searching for her. He lagged in the race, and Tiffany had no clue of the danger that surrounded her.

Chapter Twelve

Tiffany could not stop smiling. She had seen no one pass any of her dad's tests before; she had brought nobody home that her dad actually liked. *This guy is perfect*, she thought as she stared at him with her smile still plastered on her face. They drove down the road. He looked away from the road for a moment to catch her gaze.

"What is it?" he asked, returning her smile.

She just laughed and then closed her mouth to lick her dry lips and then reached into her pocket to pull out her cherry Chap Stick. Pulling the passenger side visor down to see herself in the mirror, she applied the Chap Stick as if it were lipstick and smacked her lips. It did have a slight shade, and she didn't want to have that shade in the wrong place.

"You look beautiful, you don't need to check." He smiled and said without looking at her, "and you don't need makeup."

Tiffany gave a flirty half smile and gazed at him with brilliant eyes and said, "It's Chap Stick," holding it up for him to see, "My lips are dry."

He laughed as she continued to study him from the side. She looked down in thought for a moment, and then she squinted and asked, "How did you do that back there?"

"Do what?" He answered without looking at her, turning onto the highway that would lead to the river.

"With my dad! You handled him like…" she thought, "… well, like I'd seen nobody do before. He loved you. And my mom, ha… Wow, that was a monster hit with the flowers. So sweet." She smiled and blinked flirtatiously; so natural for her it was alluring instead of annoying. Most young ladies would blink in this manner, trying to use their charms on a person to get a result. This didn't seem to faze Jason, though, for he was the one who was laying the trap in this, not her.

"Bah," he waved his hand and shrugged, "I have plenty of experience with people, especially old guys like your dad. I know what to say to get them to like me or follow my lead. You can't have a dad like mine and not learn something from him."

"But how did you know my dad would know your dad?" Her eyes were still squinting with inquisition.

He laughed, "Well, they're about the same age, so I took a shot in the dark, and emphasized the name when I said it. Just a little trick I learned long ago with name recognition." He left out the fact that Charles Adams was not his dad, but nobody around those parts knew that. Some research on the internet and anyone could find the truth.

Charles Adams took Sapling County High School to the State Championship in football in 1992, and he went to Texas A&M University on a football scholarship. He joined the army and became a colonel. He had a son named Jason, but that son died from a drug overdose six months after his dad got killed in Iraq.

These were things she didn't know, and her parents would not find out about until it was too late. So, if this guy wasn't Jason Adams, then who was he? That's the question Tiffany's dad and many others would ask, and would never find the answer.

Tiffany laughed as she again faced forward and flopped back in her seat. "He even gave you some money."

"Yeah, that was a new one by me," he also laughed, "but I will not complain."

She looked down and frowned for the first time since she left the house. "Look," she said, "why don't we get something to eat and go to the movies like I said we would? We can keep driving past the river and go to Vanilla instead. There are plenty of good places to eat there and the theater isn't bad."

He frowned, then transformed it into a sly smile. "Why, Tiffany? Are you feeling guilty about lying to your folks?" He said mockingly.

She looked down again. "A little." She frowned and sat back hard into the seat, pouting. "I just don't like those parties."

"Yeah, I know," he laughed and said, "You're a good little girl, right?" He winked at her with a look of sarcasm. "Good girls don't lie to their daddies to go to parties, especially this one. Besides, I don't want to watch a movie; we're going to the river." For the first time since she met him, Jason was curt with her, and the look on his face changed. For the first time, he didn't look like a nice guy at all. It didn't matter to Jason if they went to the party or not. It was but a distraction until he could take Tiffany to his intended destination.

"Don't make fun of me," she sulked, giving him the hurt look, her best puppy dog, pouty face. She even made her eyes get red and a little wet around the edges. Victor would have been proud, especially at her next statement. "If you're going to act like that, take me home."

"No." He glared as if he were about to go into a fit of rage for her sudden insolence. This did not go unnoticed by Tiffany, and it struck fear deep into her soul. She was being playful, but he was being quite serious. Then he sighed, shaking off his rage, realizing that he must still carry out the facade, so he gave a fake smile, "It'll be fun. All your friends will be there." He then turned on the charm and played on her sympathies. "I'm sorry, I just get intense when I drive and I am under a lot of stress. I rarely talk about my feelings with anybody, but you are just easy to talk to. It's been hard being the new guy around here. People of Beckley don't exactly accept new people openly, you know. I just thought," he paused, looking down at the steering wheel in thought, "well," he continued, "I just thought if I had the prettiest girl in the tenth grade and a cheerleader to boot with me at the party... oh, never mind." He cast his eyes down once again for effect. "Forget it," he said, "I'll take you home, or the movies, whatever you want."

Awww, he's so sweet, she thought, as she bought into his psychological bull. She looked at him with sweet pity. "Why didn't you just tell me that?" This hunk of man-flesh and his charming ways again took her in. Her eyes studied him, unwavering. With a sigh, she continued, "Why don't we go to the party for a little while and then leave?" She smiled and blinked, flirting with him again. If Victor were in the back seat, he would have been going bonkers.

Jason sighed and nodded his head, keeping the same stoic face that broke into a tiny smile on the corner of his mouth. "Okay." He nodded.

"Okay," she said with excitement, while turning to face the road again. After a quick bout of silence, she laughed again, "This is our first date, and we already had our first fight." He just nodded and kept his eyes on the road. For the rest of the trip to the river, neither of them said much, even when they arrived and got out of the car.

Tiffany could not believe how many were there. Nearly half the school was at the party, and even a few from the Christian Academy. That surprised her some. A huge bonfire roared in the middle of the sandy river beach and the different people surrounded it in groups, having separate conversations. Even though the party had just begun, at least a dozen people were drunk. Some of them probably started way early and were drunk or high when they arrived.

Someone had gone to great expense to set this up and had left nothing out. There was loud music, a lot of alcoholic beverages, cigarettes and cigars for whoever wanted them, every kind of snack. There were even a few people already jumping in the river and swimming.

Tiffany liked little of what was going on, but she shrugged and figured that she could abstain as she always did and try to enjoy spending time with friends, the music and some of the good refreshments. After being there for a little while, she got into the spirit of things and went to sweet talk with the DJ, Billy Himerman–he was in her biology class–into playing a few of her favorite songs. She may not have wanted to be there, but she would at least make the best of it.

Before she knew it, a few minutes turned into an hour and

she was having a good time. Jason presented himself as the perfect gentleman and she was famous with the girls there because she had the object of all their hearts' desires on her arm. Some of them acted jealous. She enjoyed that the most. She, like most young ladies her age, liked a lot of attention and as the epicenter of attention's storm, she reveled in it. After an hour had passed, she told Jason that she wanted to leave, and he agreed. At about eight o'clock that evening, she told a few friends they were leaving to catch the late show in Vanilla. Several of her friends saw them leave. Later, no one at the party recalled seeing them after eight o'clock.

Chapter Thirteen

Victor made it to the party, but he could find neither Tiffany nor her date. He arrived at 7:30. The overcrowded beach made it so that he didn't see how he could find anyone in that mob. Tiffany was petite and could easily disappear in a crowd, could get lost in such a group, but Victor would know her as soon as he caught a glimpse, even if from a distance. After wasting time searching, he thought, *this is hopeless; I'll never find her this way.* As he searched in desperation, he found Tiffany's friend Kessie with a small group, some of them drunk or high. Most boys had something more carnal on their minds.

The party was especially loud; the music, the fire, people talking over the music. Then with the carnal thoughts flying from some of these kids' minds that were Children of God. There had to be chaos among his fellow watchers that night, and that he wasn't the only one working overtime.

As he got a closer to the group, he overhead one say that Tiffany and Jason were going to catch a late-night movie in Vanilla, so Victor left the party and headed to Vanilla to continue his search. According to that small group, the two had just left. Victor went to the theater and wait for them to arrive. At least he could be there to follow them when they left. He would *not* lose her this time.

***

Tick Tock went the clock. Time was running out. *Time, why must we battle time?* He thought. Too much time. Panic mode set in for Victor. He looked at the faces of everyone in the theater and of those in line. The late movie ended, and there was no sign of Tiffany or Jason. Victor feared the most terrible things and thought the worst of Jason, if he could think any worse of him.

Jason could have taken Tiffany anywhere. He knew that something terrible could transpire soon and that his time was short.

Victor's only hope lay in knowing that demons loved to strike at midnight, the only time when one could be in two times or days at once. That didn't mean that the demon would hold his blood lust for that long.

The full moon gave Victor a clue what would transpire on that evening, for he knew his enemy well. Along with midnight, demons loved to make use of the full moon, playing on the superstitions that people had developed over the years. This practice dated back to the times when humans believed the moon to have mystical powers when they worshiped the full moon. This is how he knew the clock was ticking, and how little time he had left to save Tiffany's life. He not only knew when, but also knew what would happen. The realization put his anxiety and zeal to succeed into overdrive.

———

(Understanding Angels and Demons: Special Lesson)
In order for demons to survive in human form for any length of time, they had to feed their desires, their lusts, with the carnality of humankind. When not feeding on evil, they fed on fear, or worse, death, which often presented more fear than any other time. They, like the messengers and the watchers, could exist in the spiritual realm, but if they took on a solid, human form, they had to feed, to sustain that life for long periods of time as they worked in the shadows. Evil deeds could only do so much, they needed more. Fear strengthened them.

Angels get their nourishment from the powers of God in times of need when they had to sustain such form, which doesn't happen often. Demons live separated from God, so they have to take the life essence from people. This is a part of their banishment to earth and becoming defiled beings in order to keep them separate from humanity or attempting to join humanity as one of them. God took from them the ability to sustain human form. Angels, however, could sustain such a form as long as they wished or needed. They could, in extreme circumstances, transform into a human being, giving up angelic powers and properties to live out the life of a human.

Demons don't have to draw upon human emotion and energy, such as fear, lust or carnality to be on the earth. They don't have to be in human form to influence people, but it is one of their greatest tools in temptation. Some of them don't even take human form, but take the solid form. They desire the rush they receive in feeding off the life force and fears of humanity. They love carnage and death; the bloodier and more gruesome, the better. Anything that perceived as evil and despicable feeds their existence. Those who possess a human being will destroy that body from within. The inhabitance of pure evil within, if even on a limited time scale, is too much for anyone to take. When they destroy the body, they will leave and inhabit the body of another.

Two things could go on with Jason and Tiffany. Either he is a demon and wants to feed off of her essence, or there is a legion of demons occupying Jason's body, which needs to take a new host in order to stick around in that form. Either way, time worked against Tiffany and if Victor didn't find her soon, she would die, or worse.

She had one thing on her side in the second scenario. Demons cannot take a soul that is guided by the Spirit of Christ and Tiffany, although in a dark spot at the moment, remained a child of God. Unless she relinquished that power of her own free will, demons could never take her soul, but they could take her life.

Victor didn't want Tiffany to suffer any fear or pain. He is her protector, her Watcher. Not only is it his job to see to her wellbeing and keep her away from demons like Jason, but he also loved her and he didn't want her to suffer.

Tick Tock went the clock.

***

Tiffany awoke in a strange place; tied up, mouth gagged, and she lay on an old rotten, mildew-infested, splinter-ridden wooden floor. The place reeked of mold and filth, polished with eerie detriment. She could see light through the cracks. She could hear bristling water from outside. *I'm still near the river somewhere*, she thought, *but where?* Her heart pounded as if it would leap right out of her chest. Bounding. It beat so hard that she could hear it in her ears and feel it in the back of her head. Maybe the throbbing in her head came from the huge bump from being smacked there by her date. *Some date this turned out to be.* She thought with a harrumph as she squirmed to loosen her bindings.

Any exertion of energy caused her fatigue, as there is only so much air one can heave through her nose. Giving up on her struggle, she took a long and shuttered breath and released it slowly to calm herself. Then she evaluated her situation further.

My cell phone. Maybe I can reach it. The sudden realization fueled a burst of energy. With her hands tied behind her, it would be easy to reach into her back pocket, where she kept the cell phone. She struggled to no avail. She didn't have her phone.

Ugh, they must have taken it. Unless...

———

The last thing she remembered was crossing under the bridge. Jason had turned down a dirt road just past the bridge. "Where are we going?" she asked. He stared into the darkness of the peculiar road with no response. "Take me home." She said, but he still didn't respond. Anger stirred within her, and her entire countenance changed. With a small tantrum in the passenger seat, she screamed at the top of her lungs and yelled with tears streaming from her eyes, "This isn't funny. I said TAKE ME HOME!"

He looked at her, smiled and said with a sinister tone, "We love em' feisty." His eyes widened, and his face filled with a sadistic, evil grin. Tiffany rolled down the window because Jason locked the door and she failed to get out. She stretched through the window to escape. Halfway out, Jason caught her, almost crashing. *Maybe the cell phone fell out of my pocket then. Sigh. It could be anywhere; in his car, the side of the road...* Jason yanked her back into the car and forced her with his one free arm back into the seat. He reached back, grabbed something, and hit her on the back of the head. The next thing she remembered was waking up there, looking at the light through holes, and hearing the rushing water of the river nearby.

———

Perforated with fear, her eyes searched for anything that would help her escape from her predicament. She was alone in a shanty with no sign of Jason anyone else. Tears flowed from her eyes and she tried to gulp them back, but couldn't swallow from the fear. Body trembling, her mind raced, probing for what to do. *How could he do this to me? He seemed so sweet. He seemed like the perfect guy.* With the realization of what Jason had done, the handsome hunk of a man that she had been eyeing and pining over for the past few weeks became the gnarling villain in her mind.

How could she become trapped by good looks when she could have any guy that she wanted? She had them lining up to ask her out, but she had to hook the one psycho in the bunch.

Think Tiffany, try to stay calm. If you panic, it will only get worse. She thought as her eyes searched her small prison for any way of escape.

As she did this, the wood on the porch creaked. She soon heard four voices, but Tiffany only recognized the voice of Jason. Rage filled her mind at the sound of his voice. As the door groaned open, she snapped her eyes shut, hoping to give the appearance of still being knocked out. She played possum, buying herself some time to think. Fear kept her at the edge of tears, so she couldn't think at all. *Relax.* She thought, heart still drumming in her ears. The ability to relax became more difficult with each passing moment. The four men walked into the room. She didn't dare open her eyes, but she knew they stared at her. *Perverts!* She thought, *Oh God! Please... what what do they want with me?*

"Oh, yes, she'll be fine for the sacrifice." One of them, an older sounding man, said.

Sacrifice! The word echoed in her head as she tried to choke back the fear. She shook so badly that the exhalations through her nose sounded choppy. Clinching her eyes and hoping not to be noticed, she prayed, *Please, God, don't let them kill me. Please, I'll never lie again. I'm so sorry. I just want to see my daddy, to hug him and tell him I am sorry. Please.* Four men then walked out of the door.

"Do you think he'll be here by midnight?" A second voice,younger than the last, said, "because if he's not, we'll have to go on and make the sacrifice."

"Oh, he'll be here," a third voice joined in.

What do they want with me? She thought between nasal gasps and flowing tears. *What are do they mean, 'a sacrifice'? Oh, why didn't I just stay home?* Her fear turned to rage. *Jason! I can't believe I fell for that creep. What a loser! Is he the member of some satanic cult?* She continued to struggle with of her binds. She had small hands; maybe she could work her way loose from the knots around her wrists. *Maybe I can get one arm out. All I have to do is pop my thumb out of joint.* She stopped wriggling and thought. *That would hurt.* She tried it though and pulled as hard as she could, but a shock of pain shot to the shoulders and she couldn't help but to scream into her gag.

"I think our little toy is awake," a third voice said, "check on her."

The floor creaked, and the door groaned. Steps were heavy, and the person took slow, creepy strides, making the entire scene even more sinister. The room was dark, even with the light from the holes. Tiffany opened her eyes just enough to see the shadow of the man coming toward her like he was sneaking up on a critter that he wanted to capture. *Like I can go anywhere,* she thought with deep sarcasm, *'loser'.* She shook her head.

The man that entered, an enormous man that smelled like a pack of dogs, grumbled, no, growled, with his mouth closed. It sounded like a dog that was warning off another from their food. "You awake, little lady?" Tiffany's eyes popped open. She couldn't respond and just stared with fear. He walked a little closer and leaned over her, "Oh, you're a pretty one, ain't ya'?" He turned to face the door and yelled, "Ooohwee, you picked us a good one this time, Jason." He turned back to Tiffany, and bent close again, sniffed and laughed a guttural laugh, "mmm you smell good too, sweetheart." She stared at him, wide eyed, and tried to shy away from him and the smell that encompassed him. He lowered his voice and continued, "I just might need to taste you before the boss gets here." He stuck out his tongue and attempted to lick her on the cheek.

The floor squeaked, and the door moaned. Tiffany could not see past the gigantic mass of stink looming over her, but she soon discovered who had entered when she heard Jason's voice. Her mind filled with disgust just at the sound of his voice. She hated him for luring her and bringing her to that place, but the powerful sense of fear overwhelmed any other sense that she may have had, as she remembered the gravity of her situation.

"Do you really have to get that close to see if she's awake, Bob?"

Bob whipped around so fast he almost toppled over. "Don't use my name, you idiot."

"You used mine," Jason replied in a condescending tone, "but no need to worry; she won't be here much past midnight. C'mon we need to go outside and get things ready for the big guy. The rest of the group will be here soon too."

***

Victor searched roads around the highway from the towns of Lion and Vanilla and back to the river. His search covered over twenty miles in each direction. His mind stood at the edge of panic. Time ticked away and places to look narrowed. He peered up at the bright full moon, encased by ominous cloud, and sighed. The night drew cool. Midnight approached rapidly.

He wanted to close his eyes and open them to stand right next to her like he had when she had a nightmare at the age ten. If he could only be next to her like in the times of trouble, she had as an infant and he placed his finger into her tiny hand. Victor longed to be there, caressing the side of her face and head, assuring her that everything would be alright. He wished to see her eyes open and peer into his so he could again erase the awful fear that he knew she endured. To tell her, "Don't worry, Victor will make everything alright." He couldn't, and he was beside himself with anguish and encumbered with anxiety. The tension tightened as each moment passed. Rage and panic boiled from within. He raised his head to the moon and roared. Although his cry didn't present in the human realm, the bay of a coyote echoed his release. With his anguish somewhat subdued, Victor returned to his senses and, realizing the time, doubled his efforts.

At least I still have until midnight. He thought, giving him limited ease. The perception of Tiffany enduring another moment of fear and pain remained unthinkable to him. *I must rely on God.* He thought with a sigh of peace. God was the only one who loved Tiffany more than he did, and Victor knew God would not allow her to endure any more than He had prepared her. With that thought and the resulting moment of peace, Victor knew God would guide him and that He would protect Tiffany in his absence.

He trembled at the thought. My absence! I'm the worst Watcher Angel ever. The one time in her entire life that Tiffany needed me the most, I lost her. His anguish amplified as the time, too quickly for him, ticked by. His pain of loss increased.

It was his job and a privilege to protect her from harm, and until the present situation, he had been successful at it. He sulked as he watched the eerie clouds roll before the fullness of the moon, quenching the light and the safety that it might provide. For demons, the darker, the better. Then Victor shook off the negative thoughts. *She'll get through this. It wouldn't surprise him if she is amid an escape at this very moment.*

Victor walked along the highway for the third time that night - at superhuman angel speed, of course. He'd been down every road and found no sign of anything. The only one place left for him to search was the river basin on the Crypts County side.

It was a swampy area with few land masses throughout. During the seasons of heavy rain, these masses proved impossible to find. One road led into the area, but one could only reach the clearings on foot, and if the water was too high, by boat. It was a good place to hide and avoid detection. *Besides,* Victor thought, *there is nowhere else to look.*

***

The people whom Jason had brought Tiffany to were the worst kind of human beings, members of the occult, devil and demon worshipers. In this group, the leader was a demon that took human form, and a few of his demonic brothers, often in their natural form, would join on special occasions. The ritual where a young lady or young man was to be sacrificed to Satan always happened on the night of a full moon and at midnight. This they did in the hopes of "honoring" the king of devils and inviting his presence. Such a visitation would bring the ultimate glory to any sect of the occult. Groups like this had summoned up Satan, and they had written that they had received "a blessing" from his magnificence. So, the groups that performed these sacrifices, about twice a year and never twice in the same place, always hoped to call their master from the netherworld.

Many of the members of these groups were often prominent citizens in their communities: doctors, lawyers, politicians, prominent business owners; the list is endless and no one would ever know their darkest secret. Many of them were also members, even leaders, in churches. - "Wolves in sheep's clothing." - They were watchers of a totally different nature. Then there were those regular guys that were off in the head, but not bad enough to allow too much suspicion to arise. Their numbers would shock many.

Their rituals differed from time to time, place to place, and group to group. One thing that every ritual everywhere had in common; the sacrifice of a teenager. Myth says it had to be a young female, and that she would be a virgin, but that has never been true. Satan and his minions don't care if the young lady is pure, as long as she is young; a young person, male or female, at the most influential time of their lives before they entered adulthood. The reason that they use the adolescent females more often than the males is because these occult groups comprised men who were all sadistic perverts. Although, sometimes adolescent males proved just as valuable to certain groups with such appetites.

***

Victor found the road that went deep into the woods around the floodplain of the river. The area was dark, and the road curved underneath the bridge. Gloomy trees sat in the backdrop of the pale moonlight and dampness filled the air more so than anywhere else around. The perfect setting for the painting from a darkened mind and depressed nature. Victor stopped to take in the surrounding scene, sniffing into the air. Everything held a distinct sense, as if he had gone through some strange vortex into a different dimension or a different world. For the first time all night, he felt close.

As he walked down the road, he sensed something... *otherworldly*. There were demons in those woods, and he could feel them, almost smell them. Where there were demons, he presumed, there would be Jason and with him, Tiffany. As he trudged down the dark path that led to the deep marshy woods of another realm, Victor tread cautiously, but with a renewed confidence.

Chapter Fourteen

A knock at your door at a few minutes before eleven o'clock at night would be soul-stirring for anyone, but Tiffany's parents expected this visitor. But earlier, she was quite unexpected and caused a catastrophic event to occur.

———

Around eight o'clock that same evening, Heather dropped by the house, looking for Tiffany. Seeing her alone brought shock and confusion to the Brent home that hour. There stood at their door the same young lady that their daughter supposedly had a double date with. The look of astonishment told of his surprise. With his mouth agape, Tiffany's dad stood at a loss for words.

"What are you doing here?" The question sounded rude, so he caught himself and corrected his voice while shaking his head, "Sorry, I mean, aren't you supposed to be out with Tiffany and her date?"

Heather stared for a moment, shock drawn all over her face. She didn't know how to respond. A dozen thoughts or responses rolled through her mind. *What do I say?* "Uh," she replied after a bout of silence, "I thought Tiff would be at home. I mean, uh, no," she found her normal senses again.

It tempted her to cover for Tiffany, but she did not want to lie. Her watcher appreciated that. She knew that her long time Sunday school teacher and close friend would read right through her ruse, besides; she was a terrible liar. "Mike's working tonight. I, uh, noticed that Tiff seemed a little preoccupied by something today when I talked to her, so I just stopped by to see if she wanted to hang out tonight and talk maybe, but..."

Tiffany's dad's mind pivoted between rage and confusion

with the situation at hand. Heather noticed the inward battle, and it made her more anxious, which only added to the awkwardness of the situation. That she had never seen this side of her beloved Sunday school teacher didn't help matters much, either. Good thing that Tiffany's dad found out in front of Heather, whom he always respected and adored, because otherwise he would have raged and flown off the handle - and probably would have thrown or smashed something. Heather's presence and the look of utter fear on her face calmed the raging animal inside. "She's not here," he said with an intense sigh, still trying to calm the inner beast. "Apparently she lay about what she was doing tonight." He clinched his teeth as his rage increased and his entire head turned as bright red as a turnip. He stretched and turned his neck in the futile attempt to calm his fury. If he was a cartoon character, steam would have been coming out of his ears. Taking a slow, deep breath through his nose, he continued to hold the gambit of emotions and awful thoughts that ran through him at that moment in check.

"Uh, maybe I should just go and…" Heather paused because she didn't know what to say, and then she perked up a bit as she continued, "… look for her, yeah, and tell her you know the truth and she needs to come home." Her nervous countenance increased. She drooped her head, playing with the matt on the porch with her foot. She looked up at Tiffany's dad, still in the attempt to cool the flames within him. "I'm sorry," she groaned, "I didn't mean to cause any trouble."

"*You*," he emphasized in reply, "have caused no trouble at all." Wagging his head and then stretching his neck to calm himself, he continued after another sigh, "It would help us out more than you know if you would find Tiffany, because you would know better where to look than we would. I will also be looking." His brow furrowed, transforming his entire face into a menacing frown. "Tiffany had better hope you find her before I do." His face then changed to a worried, distant stare. The flux of emotions overwhelmed him. This didn't go unnoticed by Heather.

"I'm sure she is alright," she said, not sure of herself. "She probably didn't want to tell you because..."

"Because she thought I would say no. But I might have allowed it if she had been honest. I did like the boy and I don't know what she was worried about, unless..." shock and disappointment grew clear upon his face.

"Unless she was planning on doing something that you wouldn't approve of." Heather felt bad for getting Tiffany in trouble with her parents, although she hadn't really, Tiffany did that all on her own. She wondered. *Tiffany couldn't have gone to that awful party, could she? Tiff wouldn't do something like that? Oh, I hope not. I really don't want to be there, but for Tiffany's sake, I think I'd better bring her home. At least she'll be safe and away from that...* she paused in her thought to search her mind for the perfect term that would describe the disgusting things that were likely to go on... *that...* No fitting description came to her disgusted mind.

Tiffany's dad noticed the gasp that Heather didn't realize escaped and looked at her as if to inquire, but before he could ask, she said, "I think I know where she might be. I'll go looking for her now; don't worry, Mr. Brent. If she is where I think she is, I'll get her and bring her home." She waved goodbye, and for the first time in her life, Heather went to a wild party.

I can't believe I'm doing this, she thought with a sigh as she started the car and gave Mr. Brent one last wave. *But I must do what I can to get Tiffany out of this mess. Oh, wait 'til I see her. She's going to get it. Why didn't she tell me what she had planned?* Then it hit her. *The same reason she hadn't told her parents the truth; she knew I would talk her out of it.* As she drove off, Heather's mind spun in a million directions, trying to figure out what to say when she found Tiffany. After telling herself to calm down and get back to her senses, she prayed as she drove. Eyes open, of course.

By the time Heather arrived, the party by the river was in full force. Her presence did not go unnoticed, as everyone knows of her strictness in her beliefs.

She was one of the smartest in her class, sure to graduate

with honors, and was one candidate for valedictorian that year. Her vast resume, which would get her a great scholarship to whatever college she wished to attend. She knew her appearance at the party would turn some heads, drive gossip, and bring frowns. The risk of humiliation for even being seen at such a scene would be worth it if she could get her friend Tiffany out of trouble.

Most of the people there would know Tiffany. Tiffany often proved to be hard to miss. The more attention she got from others the more she pined for and since she had a magnetic personality, beautiful smile and eyes that flashed like lightning, people gave that attention to her and loved to make her smile and laugh because it was natural, beautiful and contagious.

That night, Tiffany didn't want to be noticed so much. Many had not seen her. It was odd for Tiffany to go anywhere and not get noticed. Normally, she would tease, flirt, and even joke with most that she saw. Heather went over to Billy, hard at work with his mixer and DJ equipment, and inquired of her to him.

"Yeah," he yelled over the loud music. "I saw her tonight. She was with that new guy, what's his name? Jack, James…"

"Jason."

"Yeah, that's his name. Tiffany came over and requested some songs and sweet-talked me," he blushed, "well, you know how Tiffany is, sweet-talked me into playing them for her right away. She flashed those," he paused like every other boy did when they thought about Tiffany's eyes as if he got lost in them in his mind, "eyes and…" He snapped out of the spell, "I told her I couldn't promise anything but I would do my best. She sure knows how to get her way, doesn't she? Anyway, I think I only got to play one of her songs, maybe two, and she left with that guy, uh…"

"Jason."

"Yeah! Him." Heather couldn't help but notice the jealousy in Billy's voice. Most guys, when they talk about a girl's boyfriend that they don't know very well or don't approve of, use the same voice; as if to say, "She can do better than that guy." Or "I'm better than that guy." Then, trying to play it cool, Billy changed the subject. "What are you doing here, anyway? I would never expect to see you here."

She gave an awkward smile and told him the same thing that she told everyone else. "I'm looking for Tiff."

"Oh, okay. I knew you wouldn't be here if you didn't have to be. Sorry I couldn't help you more." He yelled over the music. As Heather walked away, Billy returned to his mixer, touching the knobs and acting like he was pushing buttons and double checking everything as if he had anything to do with the way the music sounded with his actions.

Heather already worried for her friend, but when she couldn't find her at the party, she became afraid. She wondered. *Tiffany lied to her parents so that she could go to this party with a guy that she and everyone else in town hardly knew, and then when she got here, she only stayed little more than an hour. It isn't much past eight now. Where could she have gone? Maybe she got uncomfortable and talked Jason into taking her to a movie after all.*

Heather confirmed her speculations when she found a group of Tiffany's closest friends. Minutes before she arrived, Tiffany and Jason had left to go to Vanilla to see the late movie. So, with that information, Heather left the party, and not a moment too soon for her comfort. When she got in the car, she tried to shake "the Willies" off. She even tried to wipe some of the smell off of her clothes after washing her hands with antibacterial hand lotion from the glove box. She wanted to go home and take a shower, but she had a sense that there was too much to do and very little time to do it in.

She didn't know how she knew time was short; she just did. *Maybe*, she thought, *that's just worry talking*. After saying another prayer for guidance and asking forgiveness for having to carry the Holy Spirit into such an awful scene, she left for Vanilla.

***

Heather didn't know this, but when she was at the party, a certain Watcher named Victor was also there looking for

Tiffany. She had an advantage over him, though, she could ask. He had to overhear conversations and hope that the conversations were about the questions that he needed answered. Not an effective way of investigating, but at that point, it was all that he had. Of course, Divine guidance had its advantages when relied upon by him.

Later, while Victor went to the movie theater looking for Tiffany and "that rat", he recognized a face from the party; Heather. He didn't put it all together until he saw the same impatient worry on her face that he had also felt. So, God had sent some help. *Maybe she can find her,* he thought, and the next thought frightened him. And few things frightened Victor, *even if I don't.* He bowed his head in frustration. Tick Tock went the clock. Time was running out.

***

At eleven o'clock, Heather had returned to the Brent's home, and when she arrived, she noticed that a deputy sheriff's car parked in the yard. She knocked on the door and Tiffany's dad answered again. He looked like a tractor had run over him, then backed over him for good measure. What had transpired in the last three hours? She wondered, but didn't have to stretch the imagination. He looked past her in obvious hopes that she had found Tiffany and had brought her home.

Mr. Brent caught Heather's eyes with the unspoken question in his, and she replied by just shaking her head in remorse. He frowned even more than he had been, rubbing his already unkempt hair with frustration, messing it up even more. He motioned for Heather to come in, and she sat on the couch.

The deputy sheriff sat at the dining room table, leaning over to the report that he had attached to a clipboard. Tiffany's mom appeared to be a woman who had been crying for hours.

Heather's thoughts filled with fears of the worst possibilities while she sat quietly. Tiffany's dad asked if she wanted a cup of coffee or tea. She shook her head. "Coffee is fine." She did not plan to go home soon, and even if she did, she wouldn't sleep, so she may as well enjoy the coffee. When Mr. Brent brought the coffee to her, he explained why they called the deputy and what had transpired since she left to look for Tiffany.

***

Several hours before, Mr. Brent went inside, closed the door, and in a flash of rage, flat handed the wall leaving a gaping hole in the drywall. After calming himself, and his wife coming to see what had her husband in such an uproar, he replayed the events from earlier in the evening through his mind. He searched for some clue where his daughter might be and what she had gotten herself into. He questioned everything.

After much thought and telling his wife the suspicions that his mind had concluded from his deep self-inquiry, Mr. Brent went into his study and looked up Colonel Charles Adams on the internet. What he discovered shocked him even more.

Charles Adams, the one he knew, had been dead for several years. He died in the war in Iraq. Confusion and suspicions rapidly brewed into anger as he searched for Jason Adams. His heart dropped to his colon when he found an article from St. Louis, Missouri, which read, "Son of Army Colonel Dies of an Overdose."

The article had a picture of the kid and the guy that went out with Tiffany resembled him, only a little older. *Nah, it can't be the same kid,* he thought, *has to be a coincidence. Maybe the kid didn't want to say his dad was dead.* He searched some more, riding an emotional roller coaster that made him want to vomit. The more he searched, the less he found, but he found some more things that showed something strange about this boy, dead or not. After a while he convinced himself that Jason, or whoever, was not who he claimed to be. Angry with himself and heartbroken, Mr. Brent placed his face in his hands, rubbing his eyes. Sighing, he slid one hand over his mouth.

"Not only did he trick me, but..." he said to no one in particular, "I gave the chump some money." He stopped to think while pressing his hand hard against his mouth, and then he continued as if responding to himself and still talking to no one in particular, "Ha, you're the chump." He ran his fingers through his hair in frustration. "I can't believe I let them go." He chuckled in shock, "I practically pushed them out of the door." He let out a gut-wrenching growl, pushed everything off of the side of the desk and stared at the pile, huffing with rage.

His wife responded to the noise and when she saw the mess and the half-crazed man with the wild hair and eyes before her, she thought the worst and feared him, but instead of shying away, she embraced him around the waist laying her head softly on his chest helping to calm his inner beast.

"I let them go." He wept, laying his cheek on the top of her head as he held his wife close. "I can't believe I let them go, knowing nothing about the boy. What kind of dad am I, when I can't even protect my daughter?"

She gave him a moment to let it all out and then to let her know what he had found out. The worst scenarios rolled through her mind because whatever had her husband in quite a stir, it had to have been big.

He told her about what he had discovered on the computer and she listened while placing her hand over her mouth, eyes squinting with grief. Tears flowed as she listened, but she held back from crying out loud until her husband finished because she didn't want to miss anything. Then she asked, "Who is with our daughter and why would he lie about his identity?" Then her mind spun, "Oh my goodness, you don't think he'd... he wouldn't..." She wept sorely.

After a few moments of shared sorrow, one of them suggested they pray, so they got on their knees and prayed for safety for their daughter and for God to send someone to watch over their child. Little did they know someone watched over her, but because of her choices, that same someone could not be with her now. But with Victor, nothing would keep him away from getting to Tiffany, even if it meant his life. The Brent's prayer would strengthen Victor and all others on the side of good more than anyone could ever imagine.

The forces of light need the prayers of those whom they protect so that God will give them more strength.

After the prayer, they rose and called the sheriff's office to see what they needed to do. Several minutes later, the deputy arrived. Then, about an hour after that, Heather returned. After asking questions and getting as much information about the car that the kid drove, his description, the description and picture of Tiffany and other things that he needed to aid in the search, the deputy left. Shortly thereafter, so did Mr. Brent. Heather stayed to be with Mrs. Brent in her time of need.

Chapter Fifteen

The sour stench of mildew mixed with old sweat filled the air of the cabin, circulated by fear. Tiffany struggled to get free of her bonds. Muffled sounds of speech and the occasional laughter were her only company, and it gave her slight calm that she might remain alone as they spoke from a distance. They had left her alone for quite a time after the "smelly one" left. *Maybe*, she thought hopefully, *Jason wasn't really one of the bad guys. Perhaps they forced him to do this, and he was just watching out for me. Maybe he will save me before it is too late.* The thoughts of a desperate romantic, or maybe one who drew dangerously close to delirium. The door moaned and someone entered. She cast her bright eyes upon her captor, as if they were probing his mind and begging him to set her free. She tried her best to place him under her spell.

Jason had indeed been watching her, and even stalking her, for quite some time, but his intentions had never been in her greater interest. What he and the others intended for her was far from anything sweet or romantic. They did not intend to set her free in how she hoped Jason might. They planned to set her free from this life.

Her eyes begged as Jason grew closer to her. "I've been watching you for a long time," he said. Tiffany's stare drew distant for a moment as she noticed a change in Jason's voice. "I've been with you for much longer than you have known and I know your eyes, young Tiffany." *Young Tiffany?* She thought. Jason continued, "I know you use them to get what you want; to place men under your," he waved his hand in the air mockingly, "spell. You may hypnotize young human boys and tie them around your little finger with your charms, but it will not work on me." Fear again rose within her and it took all of her restraint to keep it from her eyes as she knew Jason would notice.

Human boys? She thought, *why's he talking so weird, and what's with his creepy voice? Wait, what? Watching me? He's a stalker? Who is this guy*? She squirmed as she remained unable to rein in her shock and fear. Outside of the shack, the low drone of a chant from several male voices filled the air as the men prepared for the evening's events.

"You hear that," Jason said twisting his neck and making it crack like a large twig. "they're calling for you." She stared and quivered. She tried to hold the tremors at bay, but the attempts were in vain. Her eyes drowned with fear as Jason drew close enough for her to make out his face. He didn't look the same. His eyes glowed with a faint orange tint, as if a glimmering fire flowed from within and his face had distorted; longer, larger, and gruesome. He looked like the Jason she knew, but more sinister. He reached out and stroked her face with the back of his finger, which had also changed. His nails seemed more like animal claws than fingernails; pointed. She flinched away from his approach, but could not go far as she remained tied to the floor. "Yes," he said, closing his eyes and throwing his head back, inhaling deep and holding it with euphoria like an addict getting a fix, "I can feel your fear, and see it in your eyes." He paused, inhaling deep again, fiery eyes rolling back, "It tastes so divine."

Her mind raced, finding nothing but a vacuum. Hyperventilating through her nose, she trembled all over so that it made the floor around her shake. She was so overcome with fear that it paralyzed her. Except for the tremors, she could not move. Her mind remained blank and all she could feel was the fear and sense a dark, pure evil that surrounded her. Pinned down and helpless from the darkness beyond the night, she tried to scream, but no sound came from. Not even a moan.

"But," Jason stood up so quick that he staggered. Resisting the urge to do whatever his evil mind had in it to do, he continued, "We must wait until its time. Everything is ready and everyone is here." He looked at the ceiling. "Midnight will be here soon," he laughed, "and this will all be over. You will be free from this world. If your soul is not ready, the king of this world will have you and your soul."

Who is he talking about, "king of this world"? Her mind finally opened as she got over the fear that Jason instilled in her. That is until Jason drew close to her again.

Jason should have left, but something seemed to keep him from doing so. Just what, he didn't even know. Tiffany stared at him, half in utter terror and half in mystery as he talked to himself like a man trying to talk himself out of doing something. Something evil. Something… good? *What is he pacing and mumbling about? What was he saying?* It was Tiffany's nature to be inquisitive. As Jason continued to saunter in a small rectangular pattern, Tiffany followed his every movement, staring. He kept going for the door and then back to her, mumbling and flailing his arms as if he were trying to talk himself out of or into whatever he argued with himself about. The volume of his voice rose as he continued to quarrel with himself, and Tiffany could finally understand what he was saying. "It's those eyes," he said over and over, "those eyes," and louder each time he said it. "THOSE big, blue, haunting… beautiful… EYES." He turned to her and growled, snapping his attention immediately back to the door again.

The more he walked, the more she stared. The more he mumbled and argued with himself, the less she feared. Pity for him had grown, and it showed in her gaze. When he noticed this, he stopped, looked down at her over his right shoulder, and returned her stare.

This carried an odd moment of silence, and Tiffany felt it would never end. She had never lost a staring contest in her life, but this time, she almost flinched several times, but refused to give Jason the satisfaction. The slight pity that may have been welling in her stare turned to arrogance, as she knew she had won. Her record was safe.

He broke the silence. "Those eyes," he said loud enough for

everyone to hear the pain and regret in his voice, "Why do you stare at me with those eyes?" His voice dropped, "Those beautiful, loving, and pitiful eyes." He lowered his head and then his entire countenance changed as he looked at her again, threw his face into hers and screamed with rage, "DON'T LOOK AT ME!" His breathing grew heavy as he fought against himself and he calmed down as he forced himself to walk away. "Maybe," he said as he almost stumbled. It seemed like his legs never got the message to turn. "Maybe I've been watching too close and for too long." He withdrew himself from whatever spell that he was under and staggered away, mumbling, "Those eyes."

Tiffany returned to the futile attempt to get free of her bonds. She had loosened the gag and with violent force she spat it out, allowing it to hang about her neck. Drawing a deep breath, she cried out in desperation, "Jason," her eyes pleaded, "don't do this. Please let me go." Jason stopped short of the door.

"You should have died a long time ago, you know," head hung with his voice calm. Jason didn't look back; afraid to look into her eyes again. "If you would have died when you fell from that tree, then you wouldn't be here now."

This took Tiffany aback and choked her into momentary silence. She regained her composure and then said, "How," she looked to the left in thought, "how did you know about that?"

Still not turning or moving, he replied, "Because I was there. You think the wind caused you to fall?" He sighed, "No! I pushed you." He reached up and put his hand on the doorjamb and hung his head lower.

"That was the wind, I remember; I was alone. You weren't there, no one was. That is no one but..." she didn't finish as Jason continued.

"It just felt like the wind." He still hadn't moved and his head hung low and wagged as if a war of conscience continued within him. "It was I who tried to kill you, and because I failed, you are here now."

"No," she shook her head, "but that's not right. How could that be?" She opened her mouth several times, and no words came out until, "But I lived. How could I?"

"Your Watcher," he turned to her finally, "he was there, and he saved you. He's always been there." Jason looked at the door. "Well, until now. He can't find you now because we have been blocking his senses." He mustered an evil sneer, "And I'm sure it's driving him bonkers."

Her mouth formed a silent "*w*" as if to say "why" or "what", or "who" and it all raced through her mind at once. After a moment of thought, she looked at him and sighed like she had reached a moment of realization that she already knew, "Victor!" She looked to the right in thought. "He's my Watcher?" It was both a statement and a question. Her mind still raced to understand such a revelation.

"A Watcher, an Angel sent by God to watch over you. And yes," he said with a nervous chuckle, "his name is Victor. You're not even supposed to know that he exists." He took a deep breath. "He's been with you since you were born. Well, a little before, but…" he shrugged, "I thought we got rid of him when he saved you that day. It is in the Angels' Code, an unwritten set of rules," he said in a mocking tone and flexed two fingers of each hand, "that they may never reveal themselves to those whom they are watching. To do this could bring immediate dismissal."

She squinted and shook her head again. "But why did you try to kill me?"

"To get rid of your Watcher, you see my beautiful young human with the alluring and hypnotizing eyes. We have marked you from the beginning for sacrifice at midnight on the first full moon after your sixteenth birthday. It's a trick of ours. Many of the Chosen rarely give themselves freely to God until after they are sixteen and before the age of nineteen. When we mark them and follow them, tempt them, and yes, stalk them, we keep them from doing and being good in so many ways. If we keep them from choosing Christ before they are sixteen, then Satan, the king of this world, gets their spirit to join him and us, his de-mons, in the torment of hell forever. But you… you were one of those who chose early, so we will just kill you and keep you from doing anything else for God." He said the last word with contempt and a twitch followed the word.

"With your Watcher out of the way, you would have had no protection, nor watched, or kept from doing wrong. Oh, they would have sent another, but not like Victor. Another watcher would not have cared as much. In the end, my dear blue-eyed beauty, we would have had you, or your soul." He looked around the cabin and laughed, "It looks like we have succeeded, anyway."

Tiffany could not hide her confusion at the reasoning of her being there and Jason noticed, so he explained, "My sweet, if you would have told the truth to your parents, you would not be here. They would not have let you come. If you would have talked to Heather and not lied to her about tonight, then you would not be here and you would be at home, safe and sound, snuggled up under your pink comforter with three overstuffed pillows beneath your pretty little head."

He clinched his teeth, now pointed and gnarled, as he nodded looking off to the side, "I have to give Victor a lot of credit. That was a move that I didn't expect from him, sending Heather in like that to ride your guilt. If you had not decided... well, you get the point. If any of the chances that Victor kept sending your way worked, then I would have had to have been more creative, but you made it easy." He sighed with a victorious grin. "I do like to monologue when I am winning."

"You mean?" She squinted and said in response to his monologue, ignoring the last comment, "I'm going through all of this because of a lie?"

He laughed in hysterics, losing his breath. He could give all the old B-Movie horror actors a run for their money with how menacing his laugh presented. This laugh continued for quite a long time and then stood by the door gasping for air, "Wooo... that," he said, gulping to catch his breath, "was a good one," he held up one finger with his other hand clutching his side, "woo, you're killing me," he took a deep breath and continued, "that's better. Technically, it was two lies, and you humans are all the same. *A little lie?* There is no such thing."

"You all think the lie is harmless, but it is the greatest of all the sins. It has destroyed nations, kingdoms, families and entire races of people. The perfect weapon. It seems harmless when used, but the effects are devastating and it is never alone. That's the best part. With the lie, there is always something else, and it builds into a nice pile of confusion, don't you think? One little lie, leads to one a tad bigger and then another and another. And don't forget what initially brought the lie out. If it were not wrong, then why lie about it? See the chaos? We demons so love a bit of chaos."

"Look at you, for instance. First off, you're here. Then there is Heather, she had to know you were not being honest, and your lie, or omission of the truth," he shrugged, "same thing… your lie to her got you here and by the time she found out where you went, she went to the party looking for you. Before the night is over, it may even get her here. Oh, how I love a two-for. We haven't had one of those in ages. Then there are your parents. They know by now that I am not who I said I was; unless your dad is just a complete dope… need I continue?"

"No," she shook her head, tossing her tears and lowering it in shame, "I understand."

"Good." He sucked though his teeth, smiling, and exhaled it through his nose as he walked out, "I feel better now, thanks."

Tiffany laid her head on the floor in shame. "What have I done?" she said through choked tears. "Oh, God. Please forgive me. I knew what I did was wrong and that I deserve punishment for what I have done, but I don't want to die and I hope you don't want me to. Why would you send your Son to die in my place otherwise? Please let me live so that I can ask my mom and dad and Heather to forgive me. I'm so sorry for what I have done, please help me. I won't promise that I will never sin again, Lord, but I will promise to try harder from now on, and I will definitely never forget this lesson. If You choose for me to die tonight, then that is your choice; just let me find my way to You. Thank you for your Son Jesus who took my sin away, and it is in His name that I beg forgiveness and cleansing from you, Amen."

When she opened her eyes, another shadow of a man stood over her and she didn't recognize the shape. She gasped in fear, knowing it must be time for them to take her to the sacrifice. She clinched her eyes shut, took a deep breath and thought, Okay, God, this is it. I will fear no evil for I know you are with me, your rod and your staff comfort me in the presence of my enemies and my enemies are here to kill me. You prepare a table for me...

Chapter Sixteen

Victor stood under the bridge, taking in the landscape around the river, trying to figure out which way to go when the rush of his angel sense overwhelmed him and his connection to Tiffany returned. Smiling, he knew that by some miracle time had slowed just enough in the way of his being able to go to Tiffany with no further delay. He knew she had confessed, and the confession cleansed her of the sin that had been darkening her soul. Demons such as Jason no longer had the power over her to cloud her spirit and block Victor's senses.

As sin festers in a heart, and the repercussions from it unfurl, the darkness grows. As it grows, it pushes out the light that is in there, not because the dark overpowers the light, but because the light is being snuffed out by the choice of the person who does a wrong. It is as if someone had placed the parabolic candle under the proverbial bushel and the light no longer overpowers the darkness. When the light gets snuffed out or set aside, the darkness overcomes the soul. The light of righteousness from Christ in the heart links the sense of the Watcher Angel to the Child of God. In this, the angel loses the vision.

Before the light can return, the heart must choose to confess. And, when the heart confesses and returns to the good graces of the Lord, the light illuminates so brightly that it washes out and replaces all the darkness that is around it. Victor can find Tiffany now because her light is a beacon, a strobe cast into the sky marking a place for him to land.

With a long sigh of relief, Victor closed his eyes, thought of Tiffany and...

He had taken the solid form when he appeared in the room

with Tiffany and when she opened her eyes Victor could see the utter fear in them and everything around. Shadows. *His* shadow. *What had they done to her to addle her so?* He thought. He reached for her in the attempt to bring calm to her tortured soul. At first, she wormed herself away from him but rediscovered that her bond would only let her go so far. She sighed and closed her eyes, seeming to sleep a peaceful sleep. Victor seized the opportunity to untie the ropes that bound her hands and her feet, tethering her to the floor. As she stood, he gave her a command before heading toward the door. "Go! Run!"

Without hesitation, she went. She didn't even see who it was that had untied her; frankly she didn't care, as long as she was free. She had been so ready to run; didn't even wait to see where the man who had rescued her went. Driven by fear and a sudden burst of adrenaline, she did what the man commanded her to do.

***

The hour of midnight approached, and Tiffany's mother paced the floor. The other children had been in bed for quite a while. Her mind stayed only as close to them as they slept, but strayed to the safety of her lost daughter. Not knowing anything at all is more torture than even knowing that danger lurks around every corner. No amount of solitude in that moment could ease Mrs. Brent's spirit, although she sorely prayed for such a relief.

She looked at the clock on the wall. Minutes to midnight, Tiffany's curfew. Mrs. Brent hoped upon hope that Tiffany would come home from her date, right on time, without a minute to spare, like she did every other time before, and then everything would be alright. The worried thought roared through her brain about the young man, if he was young, who had duped Tiffany into going with him wherever they were. With a gasp, she thought. *What if he was some sexual predator or worse, a kidnapper, a serial killer, or... all the above?* She shook the thoughts away, refusing to entertain them any further. At least she tried, but with every glance at the clock and the hour of Tiffany's curfew approaching, the agony would return.

The possibilities continued to ravage her worried mind. She had faith that God would deliver her child, for she had prayed without ceasing since she received that shocking news from her husband a couple hours before, but she couldn't help but to fret. *Oh, how could you lie to us, Tiffany?* She thought. *If only you were here right now and alright, I wouldn't worry about what you did or said... well, not until later anyway.*

***

Tiffany's dad had left shortly after the deputy left his house to find out what was going on. He tried to wait, but like most dads, whose *sit-and-wait* gene is defective, especially in such situations. Something needed doing, *even if it's wrong,* as he was fond of saying in such situations. He took his pistol and despite his wife's warning to wait until he calmed down and not leave in haste, or do anything that he may regret, he got in his truck and squealed off to an unknown destination.

Within the hour and after some research and questioning with some kids that he knew would find hanging out in town, he made it out to this huge secret party by the river that nobody "knew about", but everyone knew where to find it.

Mr. Brent grilled several kids in the common hangouts in town about Tiffany's whereabouts. In fear of causing trouble for Tiffany, many didn't want to talk. But when he found one of his Sunday School students, whom he knew had an enormous a crush on Tiffany since grade school, he told the boy that she might be in danger and then he reluctantly told that she went to that party with the boy. It didn't take the enraged father of six foot and 240 pounds of muscle long to find out from some others around where the party was.

With a combination of ire and fear, Mr. Brent drove to the river. On the way, he called the Sheriff's office to let them know of the party and that they should bust it up. Mumbling, grumbling, fretting and even raging, Mr. Brent drove to the party, hoping to get there before the Sheriffs arrived. But if he didn't... *I suppose she will have to get busted with the rest.* Attempting to calm his poise, he tried to pray, but to no avail.

The ringing of his cell phone interrupted his bipolar brooding. It was his wife. "Yeah!" He answered gruffly.

"Heather, just let me know..." She told him about Heather going to the party to find her and the movies in Vanilla, and Tiffany not being there or anywhere she looked. His rage remained too red to listen coherently. After she gave the information, he gave a quick, "Ok, bye!" he tossed the phone onto the seat next to him.

As the fury quelled, fear nagged at him as well. *What if she's not there and that pervert...* the thought provoked the rage again... *if he touches one hair on her head, I'm the one who's going to jail.* With that thought, he pressed the gas pedal to add to his already excessive speed.

By the time he had arrived at the river, about thirteen miles from town, he was in a near fit. If he hadn't taken a deep breath, close his eyes to ask God to help him control himself and act in a Christian manner, he may have gone into that small clearing by the river and cleaned house. But, as is often is with many things, cooler heads must prevail. So he got out of the truck and prepared to storm the beachhead.

His arrival did not go unnoticed, and the ones who noticed did not stick around to find out who the enraged man had come for. Not only was he big, he also appeared quite offended, although most of them didn't word it quite that way. After a quick search of the area, he didn't find any sign of Tiffany or the weirdo that was with her. He found her friend Kessie and several others from his Sunday School class, though. He grabbed one boy who was sober by the arm, "How did you get here and why?" He asked looking around.

"I'm the designated..." the boy began before Mr. Brent interrupted him. He knew what the boy was going to say and just didn't want to hear it or think of it in his disappointment. He raised his hand and gave a stern look that gave no option other than obedience, "Go home and do it now." The boy turned to go, but Mr. Brent stopped him, and said nodding confirmation, "I will call your parents and you and I will have a long conversation later. Now go home. If you are wise, you will tell your parents what happened tonight before someone else can."

"Is… is Tiffany okay? Is she in some sort of trouble?" The boy showed genuine concern, but Mr. Brent didn't wait to answer before returning to his previous occupation. By the time he got done with the ones that he knew there, they were all crying, saying that they were sorry, and begging him not to tell their parents. They illustrated all the symptoms of guilt brought on by being caught in the act. Through all the slurred speech and blubbering, he found out that Tiffany and that punk had left several hours before and that Heather had been there already, trying to find her.

Later, Mr. Brent realized that if he hadn't pulled the trigger on his rage too soon, he could have simply asked Heather, and he knew that she would have told him the truth. At first disappointment resulted in her not coming right out with the information, but he soon realized that his reaction put her off guard. Looking back, he could see clearly, as it too often is the case that his response to her arrival at his door must have scared her so that she didn't know what to do. *Maybe I should have said the prayer that I finally prayed by the river sooner.* Another result of reflection in such a case is the realization of the results of a wrong response. Now he had to talk to Heather as well, and apologize for his actions.

He stuck around at the river for a few more minutes, waiting for the deputy sheriff to arrive, and the gall of some kids there shocked him. Upon his arrival, some of them scrambled like roaches when a light suddenly comes on. Others he had to scold. And then there were those who went on as if they hadn't a care in the world. When the officers arrived, there were many more that scrambled, but even then, some continued as if they were doing nothing wrong. Some of them were too drunk or high to move or even care. "Uh oh," one kid laughed, "we're busted."

The bonfire had almost burned out. One deputy had called the Fire Department to send a truck to check it out just in case something should go wrong after they left.

Mr. Brent left the scene to the Sheriff's and returned his thoughts to Tiffany's whereabouts. He found himself too preoccupied with a racing mind that desperately and hopelessly searched for some kind of clue where Tiffany might be to worry about anyone else at the busted party. Knowing that the deputies would be busy for most of the night, he went on with the search alone. As he left the scene of the party, he saw the deputy that had come to his house earlier and let him know he was leaving to continue searching for his daughter.

"I will join you as soon as I can, as her being missing is my case and a priority. I just need to let the other deputies know where I will be." He answered a call on the radio and then returned his attention to Mr. Brent. "Where will I find you?"

"I don't know," Mr. Brent said, "I guess I'll start around here and then go to the movie theater in Vanilla, but I'll be around here until..." he hung his head and then reached for a piece of paper and a pen and scribbled something on it. "Here's my number. Call me when you get free here and..." He shrugged, handing the note to the deputy.

The deputy gave a reassuring look as he saw how weary Mr. Brent was. "We will find her. Keep searching and praying and I will do the same." He pulled out a pad of paper and jot down his cell number. "Call me if you find anything." He patted the man reassuringly on the shoulder.

Mr. Brent, whose head hung low still, sighed, gave a nod to the deputy and left.

***

Earlier in the cabin where Tiffany was being held, before Victor had arrived to untie and rescue her, and during the brief stints of quiet as the group outside prepared for her sacrifice, Tiffany took some time to study her surroundings inside.

If she could get loose from her bonds, which fastened her to the corner of the floor and the wall, she could escape. It amazed Tiffany that the rickety shack still stood. With all the holes in the roof and the walls, she assured herself that she would find some way out or be able to make a way through the termite-infested wood. After a nimble search, she found a small hole near the back end of the cabin that would be perfect for her escape. She struggled with her bonds. *If I could only get these ropes off and somehow get loosed from the wall.* Little did she know then, but within a few minutes, hope would arrive. After finding it useless to struggle as her captors had obviously found the only solid board in the entire shed to secure her to, again she relaxed to say a prayer.

That's when Jason returned to torture her.

Later, she opened her eyes from another prayer and psalm and saw the shadow of a figure before her. Fear consumed her. It had to have been close to midnight, so this must have been one of them coming to get her. She held her breath and said another, "God help me please," as she stared at the shadow in fear. Fear succumbed to her so that her voice had left her, and if she would have tried to scream or speak at that moment, she wouldn't have been able to do anything but let air out of her mouth. She tried to squirm away as the shadow reached behind her to loosen her ties. So he pulled away. Tiffany had no inkling that the shadow with her was there to set her free, only that the time for her to be a sacrifice in some ungodly ritual had come. Then she sighed and closed her eyes and went limp, acting as if she had fainted. The shadow stepped over her, loosened her ties and then gave her the command before he evaporated again and went out of the door unseen. "Go! Run!" Realizing that he had set her free, Tiffany didn't wait to be told again.

Chapter Seventeen

The small hole that Tiffany had seen at the back of the cabin fit just right for her ninety-pound frame. *Good thing I started exercising again.* She slipped through and found herself in a crawl-space under the small shed. She gagged at the awful stench below her, but could swallow her reflex to vomit, barely. After getting her stomach settled a bit, she surveyed the area and found nothing but trees on what appeared to be swampland. Of course, she *was* by the river, so there would be a lot of wetlands around the overflow area. It had rained little of late, which was fortunate for her; otherwise, there would be a lot more muck around for her to deal with, and the grime that she found herself in at that moment was bad enough.

From her spot beneath the pseudo cabin, she could see part of the gruesome and quite scary scene that awaited her had she not been able to escape. She wasn't quite free yet. There were about a dozen or more men around a flat concrete slab. Eight candles surrounded it; at least from her perspective. She knew the significance, or at least hazarded a guess of the numbering and thought. *The number that symbolizes infinity.* Not realizing the meaning behind the significance of the eight candles, as it no longer mattered to her, she continued with her survey of the scene.

The slab that was in the middle appeared to be some sort of altar and she noticed a gap in the center of the semicircle of candles, probably for the man to stand as he... "Gasp," she covered her mouth and hunkered down hoping and praying that no one heard her and then she thought, continuing to watch the scene unfold. *That's where the man stands for the...* She gulped back the vomit once again as her heart pounded. It took all that she had within her to fight down the fear and the urge to scream to the heavens. She covered her mouth and refused to allow herself to finish the thought, to no avail.... *the sacrifice.*

Shaking and panting like a wet dog, drenched and sullied by a ditch after a summer rain, she felt the blood rush from her face and with the thought of being hacked to pieces on that slab so that some devil worshipers could get their kicks. Her stomach continued to churn, and this time the ability to swallow back her reflex to lurch proved futile as she vomited on the ground beside her.

She tried to do so as quietly as possible, but to puke quietly proved impossible. This action didn't make her feel any better. And then her head spun. With a subconscious sigh, she fainted and her face planted into the foul mud.

***

Victor kept a safe distance. He knew about how far he could stand from the group and the demons that were present not notice him. He knew Jason had to have been looking for him because he would have been doing the same if the roles were reversed. Then Victor caught sight of Jason, standing at the edge of the small clearing, looking toward the woods that led to the dilapidated road off in the distance, which went to the bridge. He stood like a sentry, wanting and waiting for someone, daring them to approach him on his watch.

***

Jason, with his demonic presence becoming more visual with each moment closer to midnight, positioned himself in such a stance for immediate battle. He knew Victor would come, eventually. And he knew Victor would die for his precious, wide eyed Tiffany, and Jason was more than willing to provide such a service for him. He had awaited this battle for as long as he could remember, and longed to use his demonic powers and his fiery sword against such an angel. He would strike a blow for personal vengeance for every demon on the earth. Each time a demon had the chance to face an angel, they relished it because they wouldn't have to wait until *THE END*, the ultimate battle for the chance.

Every demon dreamed of a battle with an angel from heaven and delighted in the possibility that they could send one of them back. Earth was theirs, so the demons thought, and no angel from heaven belonged in their world. All they had to do was to get them to take the corporeal form and then slice them into oblivion. Of course, what Jason and other demons didn't realize was that angels were often stronger than demons, and they didn't see that truth until it was too late for them.

***

(Understanding Angels–Lesson 4)

Angels *can* die. We know them as the immortal creatures that they are, who will never die a natural death, as it will be with humanity when we ascend. Humans can't kill them, but other angels can.

Their death, of sorts, is not death in the human sense. With us, our spirit lives on when we die and how we choose to live our lives reflects on how we spend eternity. Our bodies die, but our soul and our spirit lives on. It is similar for Angels, their soul and their spirit lives on, but differently. They will no longer be available to do the work. If something were to happen to Victor on that night, he, as we know him, would die and he would return to heaven and could no longer serve in his post as a Watcher Angel. He would no longer be an Angel, but an eternal spirit. His soul and his spirit would join all the others who have entered their eternal rest. This is a time normally reserved for the great battle in *THE END* which will follow with the angels all being at rest, along with all the chosen children of God.

If a demon were to die, to cease to exist in their current form, they would immediately find exile of hell forever with no hope of reprieve or parole. That is why they roam about the earth, creating chaos, tempting and coercing humans to fail in their lives, because they too can go to hell. The demons are trying to keep the entire human race from God, and they do so one soul at a time.

In the end, Satan will lose and he, along with all of his hordes of demons and worshipers, will get tossed into the eternal pit of darkness and fire with no opportunity for escape or release. Not even for good behavior, which is not likely? The saddest part of it all is that he, his demons, and their followers will have lured billions into his trap. If he is going there, so he would think, he will not be going alone, and since the day of the fall, has worked toward that goal. He may have been defeated by God and tossed from heaven and in the end will suffer forever, but he will have struck a blow by taking most of God's beloved humans with him.

***

As Victor watched the goings on around him by the river that night, he stood in awe at the utter stupidity of some human beings. They were free and made to be even greater than the angels, yet they serve the evil and lustful desires of the flesh that were created by one to lure them away from God. If only the race of humanity could truly grasp what God intends for them to be, then maybe more would change. *If only they knew the truth.* They have been told and shown, so the choice is theirs.

Before him, several of the human participants in the ritual had donned their stereotypical satanic attire. It was almost laughable the ancient superstitions that went along with such a ruse. Victor just shook his head in annoyance as he watched the men prepare. The human in charge of the group remained ready to do the act of slaughter of the young innocent while adorned in his conventional garb. He stood in position, waiting for the young woman to come out to the great slab before him.

His chest bore a necklace made of animal teeth and spines. The stripes painted in various places on his body symbolized something ridiculous and on his lower body he wrapped himself with a cloth like a skirt and no shoes, as if to connect him to the earth, just in case Satan should come and enter into his body, possessing it. It will be some sort of honor, or at least so they would think until he actually got there. Then they would find out the truth, as their body would turn to ashes and their soul would go to hell. Oh, Satan may stay for a while and do some evil as a human, but he could only stay in such a form for so long before the body decayed.

The man had adorned head with something that appeared to be the skull of a large bull, horns included, and used as a mask. The others of the group dressed in similar fashion.

All of those taking part in the ritual always chanted in evil sounding tones as they formed in a circle around the slab, their mantra growing to a louder drone as their bloodlust rose and the last moment drew near. At the time of the sacrifice, just before the slaughter would begin, the three demons, including the master demon, appeared in their natural, demonic form, revealing all the power welcome to them in this world.

If you were the adolescent male or female who was to be the object of this ritual, all this would frighten and that is the way the ritual was. If you were even just to happen by, which has happened in times past, then you would also be stricken with a paralyzing fear at the sight, although it would be the last sight that you would ever see. Innocent or not, there were never any witnesses outside of the group. Any unlucky soul who happened upon these proceedings would suffer.

The occult group by the river stood ready at minutes to midnight. All parties were present except for one, the center of their ritual, Tiffany. The sacrifice would occur directly at midnight under the light of the full moon.

The men assigned to the task walked to the cabin to fetch the object of sacrifice and in a moment would drag her kicking and screaming to the slab on concrete to meet her doom. The more she screamed and fought, the more they like it.

Victor mustered a slight smile as they went through the door, all in a part of the ritual, because he could imagine the scene within when those men discovered their prize had escaped. He laughed out loud whenever they came running out, looking like a group of headhunters cursing and shouting about it. The head man who had been sitting cross-legged with his eyes rolled back as if trying to summon some evil presence while holding the knife in front of him chanting nonsense, paused, looked at the men, and then jumped from his seat in anger. His face became furrowed and stern and his mouth wiggled with a frown as if to form the words before he said them and the words finally came flying out of his mouth. "Find her!" He cried, "Find her now before it's too late." He glared at the moon as if it told him the exact time and cursed to himself before continuing, "Idiots!! I'm surrounded by a group of morons. FIND HER!"

They scrambled like hungry rats, searching for any morsel or some hint to send them in the right direction. Some searched the area outside of the cabin, others were inside and still others took their spears (yes, they even carried spears like some ancient tribe). One of them noticed the hole in the cabin and how it would be big enough for the girl to escape through. Two of them went to the hole from the inside while the rest of them gathered around that end of the shack. They knew she had to have been under the shack and had her surrounded. She may have escaped, but she couldn't have gone far.

Chapter Eighteen

Tiffany's father was about at his wit's end and exhausted from the search. And he had been up and down the roads in that general area, searching in and around every little nook and cranny that he could think of. He drove back and forth over the bridge that crossed the Alabaha River between Sapling and Crypts counties at least a dozen times and had searched many of the surrounding areas. He even went up toward the Nuclear Plant and the areas surrounding it and came up empty. All that he had left to do was to search the wetland areas in the overflow basin of the river. That area was all swamplands and woods, but he was desperate for fresh places to look. As he turned onto the small, single lane, rutted dirt road that went under the bridge, he said yet another quick, desperate prayer.

A flash, like something bright reflecting from his headlights, caught Mr. Brent's peripheral vision. He knew it could be one of many things, but not wishing to pass on any opportunity, if even so small. He stopped his truck, got his flashlight, and went to investigate.

After almost giving up his search and thinking that it had been nothing more than a figment of his imagination, or a small piece of glass, the beam of the flashlight caught the shiny object again with a flash and he ran to pick it up like a kid finding the most difficult item on a scavenger hunt list. He gasped and his heart sank with worry and fear, skipping a beat as he realized what he had found lying on the ground. It was a cell phone, Tiffany's cell phone.

Staring down the road into the darkness, he kneeled in the grips of fear, but a part of him had a renewed hope. At least he was getting close. Using his phone, he dialed the deputy sheriff.

***

The men surrounding the little cabin kneeled and peered into the small muddy crawl space beneath the cabin. A couple of them thought they saw something, so they dug out the mud to make it easier to crawl under there and started wriggling their way to whatever caught their eye. The ones that were inside heard what was going on. Several more went to the different sides of the small cabin to join in the hunt, while others were told to stay outside because of the lack of space and just in case the girl tried to slip past them. With all the bumping into the floor, sloshing in the mud and yelling obscenities at the girl that they thought they had found, the men made their way to the center of the cabin beneath.

By that time the headman had rid himself of the bull skull, which was now ominously lying in the center of the slab flashing from the eight candles around it. "Find her," he kept yelling, as if he couldn't think of anything else to say. He had turned into the stereotypical villain from an old television show that did not get paid for their ability to act, but because they just looked evil. In those shows, because these creepy looking guys couldn't act, directors gave them few lines. This guy's line seemed to be, and he said it again, "Find her!" He said it well.

The entire scene turned into quite an amusing show for Victor, who had just stopped laughing because he wondered, *what if Tiffany is still under there?* He didn't know why she would be, but anything was possible. So, with that, he switched to the more serious mode that he normally operated under and helped Tiffany. Searching the area, he found relief when he discovered evidence that she had indeed made it out of the cabin and was by then running to her freedom. Behind the cabin in the densely wooded area about five feet in, he found a small piece of cloth that was ripped from Tiffany's shirt.

Staring at the obvious evidence that he found rather quickly, he again laughed, shaking his head in disbelief at the bunch of rejects behind him. He then went to join Tiffany. With his sense, he popped right next to her. *All that worrying for nothing.* Then another funny thought brought his mind back to the imbeciles. He noticed that, although the moon was full and bright, the area around the cabin, and especially under it, was dark; none of those idiots had a flashlight.

***

Earlier, Tiffany pulled her face out of the mud and, with disgust and almost a reflex reaction, she wiped her muddy face with a muddy hand. "Yuck," she whispered as she tossed her hands, trying to rid herself of the grime. Her eyes grew wide with the rush of adrenaline and complete fear as she heard more commotion, more than there had been before.

She heard shuffling in the cabin above her and knew that she had better not stick around and find out what was going on so she crawled her way through the muck, pulled out from under the cabin and ran toward the only place that she could think of to run that would be the farthest away from the men and their slab of death.

As she went into the woods, she heard a guttural sounding man yelling and repeating, "Find her!" Tiffany's entire being jumped at the sound of his booming voice, and about the same time she jumped with a gasp of fear. Her shirt caught on a branch. Her heart leaped again as she thought one pervert had caught her. She stifled a scream and with the adrenaline rush from her "fight or flight" response she pulled herself free, tearing a small piece of her shirt, leaving behind evidence pointing to the direction that she had run in her escape. She didn't know that it tore but, in the hurry that she was in, didn't care.

She ran blindly at full speed through the wooded area getting smacked in the face from what seemed to be every low-hanging limb in the forest and she continued to run until she didn't think that she could run anymore or felt like she would die, and then forced herself through fear running some more. Soon she stopped by a large tree and placed her hands on her knees, gasping.

Looking around, wide eyed and afraid, she leaned against the tree. Panting, she looked back in the direction from which she had just run and was quite surprised that she could see nothing of the small encampment where she had just been.

Then she heard them. They had found the direction that she was going and pursued her. They howled and crowed like a pack of wild animals. "I see her," one of them cried, "way up there by that big tree near the next clearing." With another howl and screech, every one of her captors made chase.

With a look of disgust and disappointment, her shoulders dropped as she said, "Ugh, really?" Still gasping for air, she ran again. As the limbs smacked her some more, she could almost feel the men behind her getting closer. They sounded closer. Maybe they were just getting louder. Desperately she ran toward what she hoped would be her escape.

Soon the group had reached the small clearing where the light of the moon had shown through before, revealing Tiffany's previous position to them. They searched the surrounding area for clues of which direction she had gone. There were limbs broken in all four directions.

"How is this possible?" One of them said to another when they reported broken tree limbs in each direction. Holding out their arms, they gathered in the center of the clearing and talked for a few minutes to decide what to do next. The three demons had joined them in the search. Seeing that they didn't know which way to go, the men divided up into three groups and search in those directions.

"When you find her," the leader commanded, "howl like the demon dogs you are to let the rest of us know." He gave a menacing snarl. "It will also scare her some more, especially when she thinks we are lycanthropes." A few of them gave him a questioning stare; he frowned, sighing as he responded, "Werewolves! Lycanthropes are werewolves, you idiots. Now go. Find her!" The last phrase was in the same raised tone of the well practiced line.

Victor allowed himself another smirk as he saw that the men and few demons, which *were* demon dogs, could not figure out which direction to go because of his distraction. It amazed him that something as simple as snapping a few limbs in every direction just after Tiffany ran off proved to be enough to confuse those morons.

(Understanding demons: Special Lesson)
Demon dogs were the type of demons from which the myth of the Werewolf came from. Someone may have actually seen one before, but just like most myths of the like, the story resulted from the acts of a demon up to mischief. The same holds true for vampires and ghosts, and many other ancient myths designed to scare us. Demons live to scare. In part, it feeds them.

———

Tiffany stopped again because she could no longer breathe. God did not intend the human body to run at a sprint for so long or so far. Even adrenaline induced by fear had its limits. People could run marathons because they paced themselves, but running in a full sprint required every ounce of energy that the body could produce. Tiffany stood by another large tree in a small clearing, gripped with fear, and her heart raced. She could feel it in her jaw.

She stared into the darkness, seeing nothing; thinking that maybe she had lost them, she allowed herself a moment of peace and rest. Short-lived, for then she heard the menacing, gut-wrenching howl that was followed by a rebel yell of others. With a quick prayer, she turned again to run away.

By this time, Victor had returned to her side. As the men drew closer and as he saw Tiffany running away driven by absolute fear and the will to live, Victor slowly turned toward the ones pursuing her and with the one word in his mind, "Help." With that thought, he manifested himself in the physical world, spread his wings, and glowed with all the splendor that he could muster.

By then the others had met with the small group that had found Tiffany and drew closer to her. But he couldn't let that happen. He knew that what he did was a risk and probably against the rules, but it was something that he had to do. If he didn't do it, then these men would catch Tiffany before she made it to freedom. Although midnight had long since passed, these men were out for blood and would kill her out of spite, hatred, lust and anger. Victor shuddered to think of what they would do to her before they killed her. No, he thought, this must end NOW, and this is something that I must do. Then the men and demons, who had by then reached him, stopped at the sight. The sight of Victor and his magnificence shocked them. Then Victor commanded, "This is as far as you go, demons and worshipers of demons!" And the battle had begun.

Chapter Nineteen

Out of the corner of her eye, Tiffany saw a flash. She slowed to look up at the sky, but the clouds had cleared and there had been no sign of a storm. Then she realized that the entire area illuminated like the sunrise. She stopped; heaving for breath again. She allowed curiosity to overcome her fears enough, as she slowly turned to peer behind her. The most amazing thing she thought she would ever witness placed her in complete awe. Her jaw even hung open.

In the middle of that glow stood the image of a man with a wingspan as wide as an airplane. Tiffany knew she had to have seen an angel, and then she smiled as peace rushed over her, but she didn't know why. As she stared, one word, a name, entered her mind, *Victor.*

At first, she was a bit confused, but quickly she realized everything would be alright because... *Victor,* she thought further, nodding with self-assurance, *will make everything alright.* With her bright, genuine smile shining through the smudgy face, a smile that had not only returned to her face, but back into her eyes for the first time what seemed like months, she walked the rest of the way to the road and from there to the bridge. Another miracle welcomed her as she noticed her dad stood at the end of the road as if he had been there all along.

She ran to him with tears streaming down her face when she saw him and jumped to embrace him with her arms and legs, knocking him off balance a bit. Kissing him on the cheek she said, "I'm sorry, daddy. I'm sorry I lied to you. I'm sorry..." She stopped to weep bitterly with her face buried into his shoulder, gripping him with all her might.

He too had tears in his eyes as he held her tight, rubbing her back and reassuring her, "Shhh, now, don't worry, my doll. Daddy's here and I love you. It will be alright. I'm just glad to have you back."

"Me too," she said, muffled into her dad's shoulder. "I'm glad to be back. Daddy," she said, lifting her head to look him in the eye, "I'm never going to lie to you again."

He laughed, loving her bright eyes as she gazed at him. For a while there he thought he would never have time to stare into them again, and now he never wanted to look away. He gripped her a little tighter and put his chin on top of her head. "Let's not worry about that right now. I'm just glad to have you back." After a few more minutes of loving embrace, the two let go, and he set her on the ground. He then looked at her questioningly. "How did you get away from him?"

"Him? Oh, Jason, I almost forgot about him." She stared at the ground, deep in thought. Her father felt confused but did not interrupt, allowing her a moment to gather her thoughts. "You should say, 'how did I get away from them?'" Then she gasped, "Victor!" and looked back from where she came.

"Victor?" her father questioned, and he grew even more confused. "who's Victor? And what happened to Jason? What do you mean 'them?' How many were there?" And those were only the questions he said out loud. Dozens more raced through his head, leaving him speechless, staring with an obvious look of bewilderment.

"Jason was one of them." she had turned her attention to the deputy, who she had barely noticed until that moment. ", I think they were an occult group, you know, devil worshipers, and I was to be their sacrifice."

"Ok, slow down and start over. Now, who's Victor, honey?" Mr. Brent said as he placed his hand on her shoulder and bending to look her reassuringly in the eyes.

"Victor!" she gasped again, "oh, no, he's in trouble." She said, looking hopeful for help from her dad and the deputy. Seeing the question in her dad's eyes again, she answered his question.

"He's the one who saved me. You must help him. He was about to fight all of them by himself when I ran away."

The deputy got on his radio and called for help to take Tiffany by the arm and looking in her eye while cocking his head to one side, "Now, I know you probably don't want to go back there, but you need to show me where." She shuddered a bit and then nodded her response.

***

Victor stood, majestic, with his wings and arms spread for as long as he could, in keeping the specter of light aglow. He knew not only the demons around could see him but also by the humans that were with them and probably by Tiffany as well, but didn't seem to care at that moment. He knew that there would be a large penance to pay for this action, but to him, the risk was worth it. It was the only way that he knew of to ensure Tiffany's freedom from the approaching evil.

The demon dogs snarled and growled at the brilliance before them, pacing back and forth, blinded yet trying to focus on the silhouette in the center of the light, waiting for the proper moment to leap at the angel before them.

The men cowered in fear and were awestruck by the luminescent creature that stood before them. They would have admired his overwhelming presence if they could have, but they could not see. As the light slowly faded, the demon dogs howled, their bloodlust in anticipation of the coming battle. The window for the opportunity to strike the first blow and place the advantage on them proved small, so they must strike quickly and be on the mark.

Every demon knew any angel could defeat two demons without even breaking a sweat. So, the first strike was all important to them. They had him outnumbered by three demons and several humans to one, but the humans were a pile of cowering, fearful wrecks at the sight of the angel's glow. Hence the reason.

Victor knew that as soon as his light dimmed that the attack would come, and he prepared for the onslaught. Drawing a deep breath, he roared a warning to all who were within the sound of his voice. If the mighty lion or any other creature of nature had been there, they would have bowed to a new king.

Although startled, the demon dogs still launched their attack at the perfect moment. Victor smiled, as he knew what their response would be. He countered it with angelic precision.

One after another he beat the demon dogs aside with his mighty arms as they launched, bearing all their teeth and claws at his chest. The three of them flew one after the other in three different directions, landing with a crashing thud and rolling through the low-limbed trees with a sprawling whack. The men that were their minions still cowered, although they had regained their sight and their wits.

"Get up and fight," one of the demon dogs growled, "he's only one Angel and there is no way he can fight all of us off forever." They didn't move and stared at the demons, their faces racked with fear and their bodies frozen in disbelief. These men had seen demons and had even worshiped demons, but they had never seen a creature from heaven in all its brilliance. Now that they saw one, they felt as if they had been worshiping the wrong creatures all along.

Victor was a sight to behold in his full, solid, angelic form. Standing nearly ten feet tall, a height which he had expanded to in his full form, and having a wingspan of at least fifteen feet; his arms spread twelve. The men even noticed how handsome that he was to behold. His black locks, which were pulled back tightly against his head and hanged to just above the shoulders, seemed to glisten in the moonlight, giving him the appearance of a chiseled sculpture. His green, almost golden eyes shined with a light source from within, as if they could toss fireballs at anyone who may threaten him with a stare. And his smile, which was often present during the battle, showed not only perfection but also great confidence and poise. His chest and abs were taut beneath his olive tan skin, showing ripples of might with every movement. The mass in his arms and legs rippled with lean muscle and with unbidden strength. To the human eye, male or female, he was the perfect creature, carved and honed to excellence.

His opponents were no mere rodents themselves. They too were heavenly creatures in their originality, but they had not tasted of heavenly fruit or breathed heavenly air for generations. Demons were powerful in their own right, but the powerful presence of God and the blessing of His might rest far from them. They could stand eye to eye with any angel if they had not hunched in their wolf-like manner. Their eyes, once glowing and golden green, maybe even blue, now shone with an evil red, and their teeth were gnarling pikes drawn from their protruding jaws. Hair covered them, hiding their rippled muscles beneath. They too were quite the sight to behold. Only all beauty that they may have had at one time was far gone from them.

The greatest advantage Victor had over them was his wings. All demons when tossed into the exile of the earth had their wings stripped. If they were to have wings, then all they would have to do was take flight and be free. They were in a holding cell awaiting their day of execution, and there was no possibility of escape. Earth is their exile. The only place that they could go other than earth would be the place of eternal damnation in the pit of hell when the judgment day should come upon them.

Not all demons appeared to be the demon dogs. As pointed out earlier, some were mistaken for vampires, ghouls, and many other creatures of the night throughout the ages. They lived to terrorize and drive fear into the hearts of humanity, and they did so with everything at their disposal.

"Attack, fools!" The head demon dog growled again, "you can kill him in this form and, so attack him." The men were still staring in awe at the sight before their eyes and only attacked when one of them got nudged by one of the demon dogs. With a menacing growl, which compared to Victor's roar earlier sounded more like a mouse, the leader of the men raced toward Victor, and as soon as they got within arm,s, or wing's reach, Victor tossed them aside like swatting a horsefly.

Then the rest gathered together with the order of the demon in charge: "All at once," he said, "there is no way he can fight all of us off at the same time." With that came a simultaneous attack.

Human bodies, blood, dog hair, teeth, and demon dogs were flying everywhere. For quite a time Victor fought them off like a warrior poet, and then, as his power drained from him, they slowly overcame him by sheer numbers. The dogs were biting chunks, and the humans were stabbing their sword-like knives at his flesh. Once in a while a human or a dog would go flying only to take a slight break to shake it off and return to join the fight. Soon Victor was prey to the inevitable. With the odds at fifteen to one, they were numbers even a mighty warrior angel such as Victor could not overcome. As he dropped to the ground, the men and the demons surrounded him to gloat before going in for the final blow. Their arrogance would be their undoing.

Gasping for air in the solid form and for the first time he could remember, Victor felt pain with every breath. The demons and men laughed and pointed as he tried to push himself back up, and his arms collapsed from weakness, placing his face in the mud. Lying on the ground, he grasped at the earth, pulling with his arms and pushing with his legs to crawl away. They followed, mocking and laughing, spitting, and cursing, enjoying the moment of taunting before going in for the final blow.

Just as they had about as much fun as they could stand, they all drew back together to strike. By then, Victor was not alone. Victor, who had rolled over to his back, and with a smile pointed behind the demon dogs.

They towered over the humans, but fell short of the others behind them. As they turned, Raul slashed across the leader with his sword, taking the demon's life in one blow. Two more angels joined and the other two demon dogs would be the object of their sword's blow. The demon more commonly known as Jason, who resembled more of a ghoul than a werewolf, returned to his human form as best he could and went to his knees begging for mercy, and the angel gave it to him. He ran away and disappear into the woods. The other had lunged at the angel behind him and and his head, followed shortly by his body, fell to the ground. Raul went after the group of men, who were now trying to run away.

After quickly overtaking them, he bound them into a group with some hanging vines that grew in that area of the woods. Within moments, Raul and the other angels that were with him kneeled next to Victor, who now propped himself up on his elbows. He smiled. "What took you guys so long? You almost missed all the fun."

"Yeah," one of them laughed, "a few more minutes and you would have been dog food."

"Hardy-har-har," Victor said, reaching out, "help me up." After a bit of help and with a grunt, he was back on his feet. All his strength had left him, so he remitted to the normal state in human form. He would have to stay that way for a while until he regained enough strength to return to the spiritual realm. For all intents and purposes, Victor was now human.

When an angel got injured while in the solid form, the only way for him to heal was to remain in that solid form. It was almost like punishment for taking that form. Also, while in that form, he must endure what every human has to go through: hunger, pain and many other human drawbacks that angels never dealt with or truly understood until they found themselves in such a situation.

"I guess when I'm done healing there will be another hearing, huh?" Victor knew what sort inquiry he would soon face for his choice, but it was one that he would gladly endure, although he was in no hurry to go through it again.

Raul shook his head and responded as he placed his hand upon his shoulder, looking him in his now green eyes. "It is one that I will be more than glad to stand with you on, my friend." He nodded and smiled. "If there is such a thing as human pride for an angel, I can say that I have it today. You have taken your training and learned your lessons well, my friend. I am proud to be your mentor"

Victor smiled, grasped Raul's arm just below the elbow as Raul grabbed his. "Yes, I had an excellent teacher." With that, they both laughed and embraced.

"We must go," Raul released the hug, taking Victor by the

shoulders, and again staring him in the eyes. "You did well, my friend. Heal quickly, and then we will meet in the clouds." He smiled, "Just before we face Michael's inquisition again." He let go and turned. "Good bye, for now." Raul, with the other silent angels who helped, then faded into the darkness.

Chapter Twenty

Victor, mangled and torn, stared at the moon. The clouds that had once given a dull glow with their covering had cleared, and the orb of reflection shined brighter at that moment than it had all that night. Maybe it was the mortality that Victor had to embrace or even the sweet taste of victory. He winced as a sudden, sharp pain pierced his side. Clutching his palm to his ribs, he gasped for air. Pain rushed to and through him from everywhere to the likes that he had never felt before. Every part of his body hurt, and he did not quite understand everything that he was feeling.

He had been in human form before, but had yet to feel actual human pain. Breathing a deep sigh, he closed his eyes and smiled. Loving life and everything about it, even the pain, it made him feel… alive. With his heart at peace, his mind at rest, and as a slight cool breeze brushed across his brow, he prayed, "Thank you, Father, holy and just, for empowering me this night. If my penance is to suffer as humans suffer for a time, then so be it. It is a price that I pay without complaint. Tiffany is safe, and all is well. Thanks to you."

The rustling of the limbs from some of the surrounding trees interrupted his prayer and brought a frown to his otherwise blissful face. *No more fighting, please.* But there were no more demons or their worshipers. They had expunged the demons as far as he knew and the men all lay unconscious, tied up with vines in the middle of the small clearing where the battle had previously ensued.

The rustle caught his attention once more. He hadn't realized before how eerie the sight of the clearing had been. Now, with the moon at its full reflection, it cast a light upon the tall pines in the stretch of woods surrounding the area that led to the river on one side and the road on the other.

Trees surrounded the area, and they each cast an ominous shadow, giving the illusion of a gathering of something more sinister. With the slight wind howling above, the sound and the movement gave life to the shadows.

Calculating the rustling of someone approaching from behind, and the edgy mood that Victor kept made for a spooky moment. A man broke through the hedge of tress that Victor didn't recognize. He wore a uniform, *Sheriff, maybe,* and he had his gun drawn. When he entered the small clearing, he saw Victor and pointed the gun at him. Victor just shook his head and raised his hands as best he could. One of his arms fell to his side, limp. He noticed the pain. Then, with the thought of how things must have looked, he just shook his head. *It figures. Well, God, I guess you want me to heal in jail.*

Another rustling came from behind him as Tiffany's dad and Tiffany came into view. Victor, with his hands raised, was the first thing that they saw. Victor looked at all three of them and pointed his head to the side where the group of demon worshipers were tied up. "I think you are looking for them." Slowly the deputy turned his head and then the gun, and what he saw shocked him. He shined his flashlight at the group and gave a chuckle of unbelief.

"How in the..." he began, "well, I'll be..." he still didn't finish the thought, and then he pointed and looked at Victor in surprise, pointing at the tied-up group of men, "Did you do all this?"

Victor, with his arm still up in the air, his other still limp at his side, gave a crooked grin and shrugged his response. He lowered his arm and when the deputy didn't protest; he kept them down. Out of the corner of his eye, he caught some movement, and he turned to look to find Tiffany walking toward him. Her father protested, but she turned to give him a look of reassurance and a nod, and he let her go. Victor's heart bounded, and his breathing heaved. The closer she got, the worse it became.

He didn't understand why he was reacting this way to her approaching, but maybe it was just another of those things that he would have to get used to in his temporary seventeen-year-old shell. The first thing that he noticed when she came into full view was not the fact that mud still covered her, but that her eyes, those big beautiful hypnotic eyes, shined from the light of the full moon. Her gaze would not leave his as she approached in what to Victor seemed like slow motion. A deep ache had presented in the center of his chest, and the closer she got, the tighter it felt.

Finally, she stood in front of him and she squinted questionably, turning her cute head to one side. Even filthy, she was beautiful. Victor's heart skipped when she broke the silence without breaking her stare. "Victor?" Unable to speak because the knot that was in his chest had somehow made its way to his throat, he just nodded. She smiled and took him by his hand, turning to walk him toward the deputy and her father. Victor looked down at her hand wide eyed and smiled as she took it.

"This is Victor," she said as she approached the men and they just looked at each other, nodding, somewhat confused. "he's the one who saved me. He..." she thought. She knew she didn't want to lie again, but she could not tell the entire truth at all on this one, because they would never believe her. How Victor grew and glowed, spreading his wings and single-handedly fought off three demons and more than a dozen men as she walked to safety. "He saved me from those men. He untied me and held them back so that I could run away." She pointed to the men who were stirring, "and I don't know how he did that, but he saved me just the same."

The two men still looking at each other in disbelief turned to Victor in shock, wondering how this average sized seventeen-year-old boy fought off, overtook and tied up all those men all by himself. Not wishing to further complicate things, the deputy shrugged and said as professionally as he could muster, "Okay," he nodded, "sounds good." If he had pushed and if he had investigated for the rest of his life, the deputy would have never found out what really happened that night.

There would come a time in the future where each would think on it from time to time, and always shake their heads in disbelief. The deputy would return to Victor later and clear things up for the books, but as for taking Victor in for questioning, the deputy just didn't see the need.

Soon they were all joined by what seemed to be every deputy, every medic and every high-end figure, elected or not in the county. Those that were not tasked with taking the kids at the party, which they had by then successfully busted up to jail.

After breaking up an enormous party and then somehow thwarting a sacrifice from a demonic cult, the deputy sheriff was ready for a vacation. A much deserved one. Before the night was over, he would have told of what he saw more than a dozen times to everyone that was someone, including a few news organizations from Savannah. *What a night. How am I ever going to explain all this in the reports?*

Later he would often reflect upon that unbelievable night and wonder if anyone still believed it to be true. Why, he would shake his head. I can barely believe it myself. He would also try to figure out why all that went on in such a small town, and he would always find the same answer. It must have been the full moon.

Part 2

"I saw visions in my head while on my bed and there was a watcher, a holy one, coming down from heaven."—Daniel 4:13 NKJV

Chapter One

As the sun reached the peak of noon and the birds' chirping broke through her slumber, ripping her from strange dreams that occupied that early spring Saturday, Tiffany awoke with one question on her mind. Before she even took the time to wipe the sleep from her eyes, she asked her mother, "Have I ever talked about someone named Victor?"

After such a night that everyone had been through, especially Tiffany, the question caught her mother off guard. Tiffany's dad had told Mrs. Brent that some boy named Victor miraculously saved Tiffany. He seemed to have appeared from nowhere. But Mr. Brent was so exhausted that after releasing that lone statement of information, he drifted off into a deep sleep. It was just after two in the morning.

This left Mrs. Brent with a plethora of unanswered questions, of which she tried to begin by asking, "Who is Victor?" She found no answers that evening; only the snores of an exhausted man who had worn his mind, body, and spirit to the edge. Only when he found what he had searched so diligently for did he allow himself to rest. And rest he did. He awoke later her,that morning in the same spot.

Unlike her husband and daughter, who slept with the calmest of peace, Mrs. Brent didn't sleep at all.

Doing her Saturday chores as if nothing were going on in her life, Mrs. Brent continued to mull over everything in her mind. There were too many questions for her. It frustrated her to have no answers.

After she had lain in the bed with no resolve for hours and as the sun crept over the horizon, splashing its brilliance into the room, she gave up her quest for sleep, and started cleaning the house. Menial tasks often helped her to think.

She thought of all the terrible things that transpired in the night and knew she didn't know the half of it. This also caused her to wonder. One thing kept coming back to her in her restlessness and constant toiling to occupy her mind, "Who is Victor and where have I heard that name before?" More questions rose with the sun from that question.

Now, after hours of doing laundry, kitchen and bathroom cleaning, dusting and folding of clothes, mindless duties to pass time for Mrs. Brent, Tiffany had stirred. *Finally,* she thought with an inward sigh, *some answers to the questions that have kept me up all night.* The first thing she faced was another question. She asked the same question, "Who is Victor?"

This shouldn't have surprised her. As the Mom of the house, she had been facing tireless questions for most of her life. With the empty mind of sleeplessness and the shock of the unexpected inquiry, all Mrs. Brent could think to ask as she gave a blank stare was the old standby that mothers often used to buy a little more time to think, "What do you mean, honey?" She wiped the bar separating the kitchen from the dining room clean. Tiffany would often sit there for breakfast. Mrs. Brent went into the kitchen to pour her daughter a bowl of Captain Crunchy, Tiffany's favorite.

Tiffany rubbed her eyes, removing the sleep. She was still tired and could have gone back to bed and slept until the next day. After wiping as if she were trying to erase her eyelids, she answered behind a yawn and a stretch, "The boy who saved me, Victor, I feel like I know him; like I've known him for a long time. There is something," she turned her eyes in thought, "strange, no, familiar about him. I was wondering if I have ever talked about a boy named Victor before. It's really bothering me." Before Mrs. Brent could attempt an answer, Tiffany dove into her bowl of cereal.

It was only natural for her to wonder about Victor and all the things that transpired the night before. Any sane individual would want to forget their mysterious captor and try to learn more about their equally mysterious savior.

Her mother replied, "Funny you should ask that. I have been thinking about that most of the morning, trying to place where I had heard that name before. Something about what your father told me last night seemed familiar. Then I remembered one odd occurrence from many years ago, when you were six."

"Do you remember when you fell out of the tree by the creek and broke your arm? We knew it had to have been a miracle when we went to see the tree that you had fallen from. You should have gotten hurt much worse, or even killed. We didn't believe it when you told us where you had fallen from, but then your father got a ladder and climbed up there. We found a small piece of your shirt on that limb thirty feet above the ground."

"Yes, I remember." She scooped another spoonful of Crunchies into her mouth and then shrugged before she continued with her mouth full. "Well, sort of."

"A young man brought you me. He said that he found you by the creek. You were unconscious in his arms. I was in such a panic from the appearance of you unconscious in that boy's arms that I didn't even get his name, or even thank him when he handed you over to me. By the time I came to my senses and turned to thank the young man, he had already left. I never saw him again."

"We got his name from you at the hospital. You said it when you woke up. We later asked a couple of people around, and no one seemed to know of him. It is not a very common name. Over time, we shrugged it off as a passerby being in the right place at the right time. We soon forgot about him until now. When you said his name, we guessed he told you his name. We thought little of it except to find him to thank him, but that was not our focus on that day. We were just glad that you were okay." She smiled and placed her hand on Tiffany's cheek. "And we are glad that you are okay now. You gave us quite a scare last night."

After scarfing down her bowl of cereal, Tiffany returned to her room. Her mother's voice, which had changed to reflect the sternness of her thoughts, stopped her. "Just a minute, young lady. Have a seat." Tiffany cringed as she returned to her seat. She knew what was coming. "There is still the matter of your actions over the past few days."

Yep, she thought, *here it comes.* Her mother left her alone for a moment as she went and retrieved her father. He was on the computer trying to find out as much as he could about this boy named Jason, and now a boy named Victor. He had been pouring coffee into himself since he had gotten up.

When the parents returned, they all had a thorough discussion about what Tiffany had done, the importance of honesty. They pointed out how none of what had happened would have happened had she just told the truth. Although they were praising God that she was okay, things could have turned out much worse than they did.

They told her how she had worried them, that she breached their trust and how she should not trust every good-looking boy who gave attention to her. She was raised better than that, and the list of stereotypic lectures that fit the situation rolled on.

Tiffany knew everything that they were going to say, and she didn't argue or fight against them. She took it as they harangued for over an hour. She knew that she had acted wrong, and that she deserved whatever punishment that they planned on handing over to her and more. After settling on a punishment that was probably too lenient to fit her many crimes, they dismissed her to return to her room and read the scripture verses that they had given to her to meditate upon and pray over. She was told to focus on what had happened to her and what she could have done to prevent it.

***

Several weeks went by. Not a day or evening had passed where Tiffany did not mull over the mystery that was Victor. She felt she had to find out who he was and why he seemed so familiar. Was he the same boy who saved her all those years ago, only to return to save her again? *No,* she would shake her head; *it can't be the same person. That's impossible. Get a grip on yourself,*

Tiffany. Then, after further thought. *Can it be?*

What she saw that night was impossible. *Had I imagined the glow and later the men all tied in a nice bundle for the sheriffs to take into custody? All that was missing was a big red bow.* Maybe she was so struck with fear that her mind built an apparition out of a boy that showed up to help her and gave her hope. Maybe, maybe, maybe… the more she thought about it, the more questions and maybe's she found.

Tiffany had many dreams. Often, they would end with her screaming herself awake. Sometimes, though, they would end with her turning to see a glowing figure spreading his wings, readying himself to keep her safe. She would lie in her room at night and cry. Her parents took notice of this as they checked on her, but they didn't know what to do any more than she did. They would just hold her and love her and pray with her until the moments passed.

Soon Tiffany returned to school. After such an ordeal, she needed a few weeks to clear her head. She did her school assignments from home. Before returning, she knew she had to be prepared for a barrage of questions from everyone, and did her best to ready herself for the onslaught. They didn't disappoint.

They tried to be caring, but curiosity got the best of them and they had to know what happened first hand, often coming off star struck in their approach. This gave an air of an insensitive nature on their parts. It didn't seem purposeful or some sadistic need for them to feed on Tiffany's pain, but the overwhelming need for gossip and drama seemed to pique their interest.

"What was it like being kidnapped?" Most who saw her on her first day would ask the same questions in the same way. Jovial excitement, like they might act when discussing the popular TV show. The same lust for blood and guts that made the books and scary movies exciting, made what happened to Tiffany the same for them.

"Were they really demons, or guys dressed up like them? Did they look like they do in the movies? The wolf-like creatures. Were they like the werewolves in the old movies or the new ones? What about the vampire looking guy, Jason? Did he try to bite your neck?"

On and on the questions went and more and more Tiffany detested her so-called friends, who had somehow taken her time of pain and immortalized it and her with it. They stayed in awe of the entire situation, as if they thought the whole thing was cool. Some had even said they were jealous and almost wished it had happened to them.

To this ridiculous sentiment, Tiffany simply smiled, wagged her head and said, "No, you don't." *If they only knew the truth,* she continued in thought, *the terror; the pain; the fear.* And she could have continued the mental torment. That unexplainable anguish that came from the not knowing if you would ever see your mother and father or anyone on this earth again.

The utter guilt would come from the realization that the last thing your parents, those who loved you the most in the world, who had been your protectors and providers for your sixteen years of life, held within their minds, the last memory of their daughter, was a lie. Then came the regret, fear that she could never make it right, apologize, and receive forgiveness. The self-loathing followed and, from that, the feeling of pure foolishness, of giving in and wishing for death, just so it would all end.

No, she thought as her false smile, the one that she used when she wished to appease others, to appear unfazed by their reproach. *You definitely don't.* The conversation would end with a gaze into nothingness and a sigh. Getting the hint, she dropped the subject and left it alone. She cherished and embraced those moments. She knew they would be few.

Even while at school Tiffany couldn't help but to wonder about the fate of Victor, and the mystery of his nature. *How did he know to help me? Where did he come from? And how did he take down all those men?* She had to know. Until she did, it would haunt her even in her dreams.

As she thought of that night when her Angel glowed to protect her, she felt at peace. This would always overcome her fear. Victor was her knight in shining armor, her knight of light, the one who warded off those who would have brought her death. He risked his life for hers and in the process took quite a beating and sustained many injuries on her behalf.

She stared *through* the wall, not seeing it, and the memory forever etched in her mind carried her away in a waking dream. Her surroundings faded into the glow of the memory of her protector and champion. Placing her hand on her cheek with a sigh, she thought, *and he's monster fine too.*

Her moment of solace ended when Kessie, who couldn't wait to get all the juice on what happened first hand, joined her for lunch. So, with another sigh of a different sort, Tiffany endured her ramblings, but only heard her own thoughts. *If only this day would just end.*

***

Victor, now in the flesh until the injuries that he received while fighting healed, lay in a hospital bed in an empty room, alone. He was tired, in pain, hungry, and mentally drained from the constant barrage of questions from the investigator from the Sheriff's office.

"Why were you there, and how did you know to go there? Where are you from? Who are you?" The questions went on and on. Victor had few answers.

He could answer the first, but the others posed quite a problem. He couldn't tell them, "Well, I'm Victor, that's it. No last name, just Victor, and I am a Watcher Angel. Oh, and I'm from heaven, you know, where Angels are from." If he had done that, he would have spent his time of healing in a psych ward somewhere, doped up on Haldol staring at the walls and rocking, mumbling to himself, and wondering if his true reality was true or just a figment of his schizophrenic mind. No, he just took the safe route and used his alter ego.

(Understanding Angels–lesson 5)

A part of the training at the Watcher academy was for the contingency that one would have to remain in corporeal, human form for an extended time. Although taking this form for most reasons infracted the rules, sometimes it was warranted and even recommended. Once in human form, they must suffer the consequences, such as remaining that way until healed, which could be torture. Then, when they resume the angelic form, there would be an inquiry.

As a part of the preparation, they formed an identity in case Angels stayed human for a time.

———

In this respect, Raul had prepared properly, and Victor's cover ID checked out. It satisfied the investigator.

Then there was the matter of Jason, the one who had gotten away. The investigators used the information that Victor and Tiffany gave. Jason seemed to have disappeared into thin air. This did not surprise Victor.

He knew they would not find that Jason. He also knew that Jason would return. Jason had a job to do. A demon ghoul always succeeds or dies trying. The thought of Jason being out there somewhere kept Victor on edge. It was yet another emotion and byproduct of temporary humanity that annoyed him. This worry brought many questions to Victor's mind.

What if Jason returned before he was ready to protect Tiffany again?

What if he came while he was in the hospital?

What if he kidnapped Tiffany again?

What if, what if, what if...? The self-torture had no end for Victor.

After several weeks, he could leave the hospital. Even his training on time in the academy couldn't train him for that awful test. Upon his release, Victor stepped right back into the role that he had performed every day since he came to earth. He found Tiffany and watched her. Only this time it was different, because he couldn't watch her from wherever he wanted. He had to watch her from a distance.

A part of him hoped she wouldn't see him, *the whole weird stalker thing.* Then there was that part of him that always hoped that she would; that part of his angel's heart that longed for her to know him as he had known her for so long; that part that adored her without pause.

Since he had held her in his arms, all those years ago, and looked into her eyes from one human to another, he had secretly longed to hold her once again. He knew he shouldn't, but now that he was in human form... *Oh, it still isn't right. I am her watcher.* An argument with himself that often raged, and the longer he remained in human form, the worse it became. *Human emotions are going to be the death of me.*

Victor was receiving a crash course on what it meant to be human. He knew the emotion of love, but had never felt it so savagely. He didn't know what to do with it. The anxiety alone threatened to drive him insane.

Toward the end of the school day, Victor stood on the sidewalk across the street. It was a warm spring afternoon with enough clouds in the sky to keep the rays of the sun from a direct assault. Victor could smell the fresh grass clippings, a soothing aroma of spring, and for one without an allergy to them, relaxing. Victor hadn't been a human long enough to develop such afflictions. Why, if he were to sneeze, he would think his brains were coming out.

It was difficult for him to see because of the parents that lined up to pick up their children at the High School and the Elementary/Primary complex right next door. A uniformed officer had pulled up, turning on his flashing emergency lights to direct traffic. For only a moment. Silence ruled the scene. The occasional car would zip by, but nowhere near as fast as it normally would because of the presence of the police officer.

The odd silence ticked away as everyone, Victor, the cars in line and even the officer waited for the bell to ring, unleashing a scene, starting with the exodus of students pouring out of school. One could almost imagine that the building was sick, regurgitating every out. Buses lined up in the back and they would soon pour out in a sea of orange in all areas of the city and county, taking the students home. Students who drove to school would reach their cars, and after a moment of casual conversation about where to meet and what to do later, their cars would roar to life. Soon they too would join the symphony of chaos. Then there were those who walked home. They lived close enough to the school to not ride the bus, and their parents didn't have to come and pick them up.

Because Victor knew Tiffany better than himself, especially in his current situation, he knew she would walk home. He also knew that she would cross the street right where the traffic cop stood, bringing a small bit of order to the chaos that occupied the short stretch of highway in front of the school. Then she would turn on the sidewalk to proceed home. Victor stood in the exact spot on the sidewalk where she would turn to go home. He wished to meet her face to face.

His heart pounded with anticipation and anxiety as the bell rang and he craned his head over the traffic, bouncing to see the front doors of the school, hoping to find Tiffany. He also hoped that she would somehow recognize him, and if she did, that she wouldn't ignore him, or at least not avoid him. But again, he knew his Tiffany, and he knew she would not be rude. Even if she was a little uncomfortable, she wouldn't let it show. But in Victor's quickly "becoming human" mind, a haunting thought remained. *What if she ignores me and walks on by?*

Then the moment had arrived, and when he saw her, Victor's heart stuttered and a lump grew in his throat, along with the tightness in his chest. He still didn't understand this sensation. He had the same longing that every boy and girl in the world felt when they saw the one that they pined for approaching. He sighed as she walked toward his way, realizing that the moment he had awaited all day had come. Sweat poured from his palms, a sensation which he didn't notice until he lifted them to swat a gnat. He wiped them on his shirt. The bounding in his chest increased as she drew closer and as he wondered what she would do upon seeing him. He noticed he had been holding his breath and forced a deep one to relieve the stress. His suffering eased when he caught her eye, and she smiled. For a moment, Victor's heart stopped. Somehow, he knew everything would be alright, at least for that moment, anyway.

***

When the bell rang, signifying the end of the day, Tiffany couldn't leave that school fast enough. She sighed with relief as she walked through the front door. *Finally, an end to one of the worst days of my life.* A day she never wanted to relive.

All the inquisitions, the sudden fame; she had already been popular, but now everyone knew her. She didn't want to be known this way. No one did. It seemed like an anvil lifted from her shoulders as she walked away. It grew lighter the farther away from the school she walked. On previous days, she walked home with one or two of her friends, but that day she didn't want to wait and meet them. She wanted to stay away from everyone; she just wanted peace.

As she approached the road, waiting to cross the street, she saw Victor standing there, watching her. He had just gotten out of the hospital She didn't know the extent of his injuries until that moment.

His arm was in a sling, and he had a cane. She looked down at the cast on his left foot. He had a few scrapes and bruises on his arms and his face, and he had his ribs wrapped. But she couldn't know there from a distance. He had many stitches from the deep gashes he sustained in the fight. He looked like he had gone through a meat grinder. Tiffany couldn't help but smile as she saw him.

He was a breath of fresh air and the only person she wanted to see. She winced a bit at his appearance, but it only increased her pity. She needed to focus on someone else, hear someone else's story for a change. *Lord knows I've told mine enough today.* She rolled her eyes and sighed.

Her Victor, she thought as she looked at him. *The good-looking, mysterious young man who saved my life.* The thought plastered a smile on her face. Then she remembered the last mystifying boy that caught her eye, and she thought she had learned her lesson. Yet there she was, about to cross the street to walk home with another mysterious stranger, cute, but still a stranger. Somehow, though, she knew this time it would be okay.

She didn't know him, really, but there was something familiar about him. She felt like she had known him for her entire life.

Of course, Victor would never harm Tiffany. She was his life, but remained unaware. She joined him on the sidewalk and they exchanged niceties and they began their walk to Tiffany's home. Although Victor had walked Tiffany home before, for the first time, Tiffany knew of his presence. As they walked, they talked. They wouldn't get into the deep stuff until they sat on her front porch a few minutes later and Tiffany would then learn the truth.

Although everything about his fallback identity as a seventeen-year-old kid from Tennessee was good enough for the Sheriff and everyone else, Victor did not wish to hide himself from Tiffany any longer. He knew he could never look at her and not reveal everything to her. That was what he intended to do. Reveal everything. There may be consequences for his actions. This would come up at his hearing. Maybe because of human emotions or because he could give up, he just didn't seem to care. Tiffany had been through enough. He decided it was time for her to find out who Victor truly was.

Chapter Two

They sat in silence on the stoop under the carport. The night air was cool and comforting. The setting sun shot through the clouds with a pink hue. They both sat in nervous silence, enjoying the beauty of creation, and neither wanted the serenity of the scene to end. They began with small talk, music, movies, and of course, Victor liked everything that Tiffany liked.

Tiffany asked questions that had raided her subconscious life for so long, beginning with, "Who are you?" Although he told her of the official identity, Victor Simpson, who came from Tennessee and seventeen years old, he also told her of his true nature. He thought about sticking to his false identity, but as soon as he took one look at her questioning eyes, which told him of questions that she longed to ask, but didn't know how, he told her the truth; all of it, even at the risk of sounding crazy. Without having to ask, Tiffany received an answer to all of her questions.

At first, she was skeptical, confused, reluctant, and even a tad freaked out. Once he gave a few examples from her life that no one, not even her parents, could know. She believed him. But she still found the entire situation a bit off-putting, and it took a little work for Victor to convince her he wasn't just some pervert who had been stalking her for years. She had already been down that road and refused to travel down it again. Imagine finding out suddenly that for your entire life, you have never really been alone, even when you thought you were. It could frighten, or at least disconcerting.

As Victor continued to spill everything to her like a river that had breached the levy, Tiffany trusted him more. In her mind he glowed, like he had done several nights before. He couldn't glow, of course, because his injuries had stripped his power from him. She stared at him, questioning but loving as he told her the things he knew of her and saw in her. Love seemed to ooze from him like the aura that surrounded him in her imagination. She was enrapt in him and his words, the more he spoke, the more she accepted he was indeed an Angel sent by God. One sent to watch, guard, direct in secret and to love. Then he explained his greatest pain. It broke her heart so that she only thought about her response, *All those years? She swallowed hard and said it.*

With a deep sigh and a drawn face, Victor began with a simple question. "Do you know what unrequited love is?" With this question, he planned to explain his deep-rooted love for her; a perfect love.

"Yes." She nodded, seeming to stare into him instead of at him. Her smile faded. "It's when you love someone and they don't love you in return."

"Or even know that you exist," Victor added, as he returned her gaze with sorrow. Realization slapped Tiffany like a wave crashing upon a rocky shore and kept coming. She stared in awe and in pain for him as the emotions rushed at her too fast to control. He noticed her shock and said, "Yes," he said, "I can see that you are understanding. I have been your Watcher since the day you were born, and the moment I first looked into your precious eyes, the moment you took my finger into your tiny hand, I was lost in you. I know how a father feels with his children, how a mother feels when she first holds her child, or how God the Father even feels when one of His children pledges their lives to Him."

"Then I watched you grow, always there, just in case anything went awry, protecting and watching you. I knew your greatest desires and wildest dreams, while not allowing myself to know your thoughts, because those remain yours alone. I learned to read them, though," he pointed to her eyes, "in there. Oh, yes," he smiled at the sudden change in her face and continued, "I can almost always know what you are thinking." He looked to one side, as if debating what he wished to say next. He sighed and said, "I may not get into your mind, but you have always been in mine."

"I know what time you go to bed and how long it takes for you to go to sleep. I know you in ways that only God in heaven knows, and I understand why He loves His children so much. There is only one that I love so intimately, but He has billions. I have loved you with the perfect love, a love just like God's love, a love that pales compared to any other, yet," tears welled in his eyes and rolled down his cheeks, "you never knew that I existed," he sighed and wiped his eyes, "that is until now. Other than God himself, no one has loved you more than I. You are my Tiffany. It's an awful drawback of having such a job as mine. There is no training in any academy that can prepare anyone for the pain of unrequited love. A part of me knows how God feels when people refuse to know that He exists."

He draped his head. Tears dripped from his eyes. She lifted his head by the chin and opened her mouth to say something, *anything;* she thought. She longed to sooth the pain Victor had harbored for so long, but the words did not come. Seeing that in her eyes, he continued for her. He lifted his head with an understanding smile, for he knew that she still didn't quite understand.

He took her hand into his, inhaling deeply and slowly exhaling with the closed eyes of elation. "Imagine a father who has a child that is incapable of love, or returning his love. It would torture him because he wants to hold her when she is sad, but cannot. He wants to pet her when and injuries hurts her, but she won't let him touch her. He longs to rock her to sleep on nights that she cannot sleep, but cannot come near her in fear that she wouldn't understand."

"This father would live in misery because he loves his child, and she is right before him, but it is as if he were just any other person to her. Oh, he may feed her, and care for her, giving her what she needs, but in no way does she ever return his great love, because she can't; she is truly incapable because she doesn't know how."

"Now, change the scenario and imagine someone you cannot see and the object of his affection doesn't even realize that he exists. That is my pain. I have loved you from the beginning, but there was no way for you to understand that or for me to show you. No way to hold you when you were sad, pet you when you were in pain or rock you to sleep when you lay awake at night, unable to sleep. I've always been there, but you never knew."

"Even now, as I look deep into your eyes, I know you still don't understand this love. How can you? How can I explain it so that you can completely understand?" He sighed, lowering his head again. "How do I show you with words that the perfect love, the love of God, the love of Christ is the same way I love you?"

His heart no longer drummed as it had when he first spoke, and his hands were not sweaty or shaking, and his feet were no longer cold. He and Tiffany stared at each other in silence. Victor studying her to see if she may have an inkling of understanding. She tried to figure out what to say, and then with a spark of realization, Tiffany broke the silence, "For God so loved the world," she squinted with her head cocked to one side like a Cocker Spaniel inquiring, "that he gave His only begotten Son…"

Victor nodded and smiled as she smiled, almost shocking herself. *She's got it, she understands the perfect love.* Victor replied, "Greater love has no man than this…" he smiled.

"That he gives his life for a friend," she smiled, "so Jesus loved me so much that He gave up everything for me, even when I wouldn't or couldn't return that love. That is how God loves us. I have always known that, but never understood it so vividly. Christ came to die for us so that we could return God's love. So, what you are saying is that you have loved me, and still love me with perfect love. Do you not love everyone this way?"

"No," he wagged his head, "only God can love everyone in that deep, perfect love. Humans can love one other in that way, but they must know them intimately, in holy matrimony. I have love for my fellow angels, my mentor especially, but even he and I do not share the love that God has for all."

"We watchers have a special duty and we know one particular human better than anyone, so we love them without flaw. God knows everything about us and He is the only one who can, so His love for us all is absolute. Why, He even knows us better than we know ourselves. You will one day love one man more than life itself, and would give your life to and for Him. When you do this, you will understand this type of love, but only partly. Unlike God, we cannot know everything about everyone all the time, but we can learn to love like Him."

"I had a taste of that with you. There is no one in the world or in the heavens that I know better or love more. That love cannot be returned, and I understand that. It's a byproduct of my job. But we can all love this way, humans and angels alike, if we just open our hearts and let ourselves love with that perfect love of God. It sounds simple, but too often the flaws of humanity get in the way."

Tiffany peered off. to the side in thought. Seeing that she had again become troubled, Victor placed his hands on her upper arms and winced as a sharp pain reminded him of the sling and injury to his arm. This stirred her so that she returned her gaze to him. She looked at his hands on her arms and then pulled her eyes up to his. "You have had boyfriends," Victor said. This wasn't a question. He knew the answer, so he didn't wait. "You had feelings for them, a crush, and you may have thought it to be love, but it wasn't. Strong feelings; euphoria maybe, but not love. Now compare that to how you felt when you first saw your daddy after you escaped from the demon worshipers."

Tiffany remembered running to him and jumping into his arms and how he embraced her and refused to let her go. She felt safe in his arms, loved and loving. She never realized how much she loved her daddy and how much he loved her. Her eyes welled with tears; they glistened from the moisture. Victor gave a reassuring smile and nodded, for he knew that the light bulb of realization had flickered in her mind.

"Now, that's the perfect love that I am talking about. Your daddy would have done anything, given everything, just to hold you in his arms again. That is also exactly how God loves you and how I love you. Only..." his head dropped and his smile disappeared, "only, I..." he hesitated, shifting his eyes from side to side, seeking the right words.

She smiled and finished it for him. "Only you thought you could never feel the warmth of my embrace." With a sweet countenance, she pulled his face up so he could see her eye. She leaned toward him. He recoiled somewhat, but she persisted slowly in laying her head on his shoulder, giving him a passionate embrace. With her face next to his cheek, she pursed her lips and gave him a soft kiss, and then rested her head on his shoulder. He didn't return her hug at first. He had no clue how to respond. But remembering what he had seen in times past, he returned her embrace as best he could with one arm, placed his cheek on her head, and wept. For the first time in his existence, Victor, who had given so much love, felt love's warm embrace.

***

Victor and Tiffany stayed outside and talked until her mother came out and told her it was time for her to go to bed. She had introduced Victor to her parents when they got home from work, and her father just gave them both a strange, thoughtful look. Without saying a word, he went inside. When Tiffany's mother came and told her to get ready for bed, Victor excused himself and then walked to his temporary home. The one thing that Victor didn't tell Tiffany about himself that evening was where he had stayed while he remained in human form.

Another drawback of being in the human form, Victor could no longer sense other angels or demons. While he walked home that evening to his temporary abode, that realization hit him and he felt a new sensation in his never-ending discovery of the perils of humanity. He experienced a new form of anxiety that he had never felt before, fear. He was alone, had a broken arm, torn shoulder muscle, a broken ankle and nearly fifty stitches, and no longer had the body of an angel, but that of a seventeen-year-old boy. If the demons wished to finish him, then he would be helpless to defend himself. *If only I had a watcher,* he thought, chuckling, *then everything would be alright.* He looked up, "You're going to have to protect me, Lord." He hobbled on down the road. The street was dark. The soft breeze in the trees that earlier gave a romantic scene to a beautiful sunset now cast sinister shadows from the light of the rising moon.

God answered his prayer long before he even prayed it. His old mentor, Raul, stood close by and he just smiled as he heard Victor's prayer. Victor should have known someone would be there for him, that he wouldn't be defenseless and alone. Raul had a temporary assignment to assist and protect Victor until he healed. As a part of this duty, Raul had to watch over Tiffany as well. He could handle it.

Chapter Three

As the darkened night succumbed to the rising of the moon, another watched Victor from afar. Jason hid well, but Raul still sensed his presence. He kept his essence hidden from Jason, for Raul could protect Tiffany and Victor better if Jason did not know that he was there. And Jason didn't.

Roosted up in a tree in the yard outside of Tiffany's window, Jason watched Tiffany and her house. Several days he spent in waiting for the right moment, plotting and scheming. As much as Victor loved Tiffany, Jason hated her more. Thoughts of her demise at his hand and that of his nemesis, Victor, fueled his rage.

Jason's feelings conflicted with Tiffany; infatuation and a loathing and malignant. Now Victor, he just held complete disdain for and relished the day that he would rid the earth of him. But Tiffany... This conflicted mindset took his animosity to higher levels. His craving grew more carnal and hedonistic. He fought against himself as much as with those objects of his rage. In his own strange way, Jason was in love with her. Filled with lust and rage and some sick need for revenge, Jason scowled at the window outside of Tiffany's room.

He held the same look of contempt as he watched Victor, his now mortal enemy, walk down the street to his hidden place to lick his wounds. *Your time is coming soon, Victor.* He was no longer just bent on mischief, but motivated by vengeance. They made him an incompetent fool, and he would not stand for it. Victor would pay with his feeble, little frail and human life. *Now that he is human, I will tempt him, destroy him, and drag his soul to hell. Then I will destroy Tiffany's life, making her my little pet.*

Jason seemed to enjoy plotting from the limbs of trees. It was, in fact, his first act of mischief when he pushed the young Tiffany from the high hanging limb, making it appear as if the wind had knocked her off balance. *Ha,* he sneered with reminiscence. *Nobody even knew the difference. You should have seen the look on your face, Victor. You were like a scared little girl yourself. What a wuss. Ha,* he looked over at the road and then back to the window. His head stooped, but his eyes cut upwards to glare into Tiffany's window.

His appearance had changed, like that of a large buzzard, a ghoulish physique, with the orange/yellow eyes and pale, almost green skin. The disguise as a human boy morphed as he slipped into the slow fade to the evil, gnarled form of a demon. His twisted face and molting body matched the intentions of his heart. *Wait 'til you see what I do next.* He threw his head back and laughed at his own musings, having no audience but himself. He hoped someone heard his howl in the dark of night. A nearby dog barked in response and whimpered when Jason growled back.

———

(Understanding demons: Lesson 1)

We can now reveal more about the demon known as Jason than previously shown. Jason is the name that a demon took for himself when he was in human form. His proper name doesn't impact the telling of this story.

No matter how he appeared before, his true self came to light on that night. As the mask and the facade of humanity slid away, the demon known as Jason revealed.

Humans would classify him as a ghoul. Some would say that he favors the mythical vampire. That would be an accurate description of him and his type of demon. Sometimes, as seen earlier, he would present as a demon dog, or appear to others as a werewolf, a creature of the full moon. This was all done to garnish fear and gain power over humanity.

In order to remain in human form for extreme periods and keep his link to the spiritual world, a ghoul must feed off the spiritual essence of human beings. Demons feed off of the times when humans perform evil acts. The more heinous the action, the more power they draw from it. Death gives them the greatest pleasure, so getting human beings to maim, kill and destroy others is what they love to do the most.

Many would come for the worst acts and revel in the feast of carnality. Then when they are done with the humans that they have tricked into acting on their behalf, they kill them, getting one last feed from their soul before dragging it to hell.

While in the human form, Jason could go anywhere appearing to be human. In the state he was in that evening, he could only skulk in the darkness and stalk his prey from the shadows. Jason and the like are bad guys of the worst sort. They have nothing in mind but chaos, pain and death for anyone born of this world. They have one goal that has remained since the beginning, to destroy the souls and lives of humanity. Even those who worship them will perish with the rest. Satan and his horde go to great lengths to make themselves appear harmless, or even as one of the good guys, but they are nothing but the angels who had fallen from heaven never to return. Their vengeance against God comes from destroying his children and taking us with them into the eternal torment that awaits them at the end of the age, hell.

———

Jason sat high on his perch that dark evening with no moon in the sky. He leered at the window, lusting for the feed that Victor had robbed him of and plotting his vengeance. A cat climbed next to him and rubbed up against his side, purring. He looked down at the creature with a start. After a quick moment of surprise, he realized the creature and with a distaste for all the creatures of the earth, he flicked his wrist and smiled as the cat plummeted some forty feet to the ground, "Let's see you land on your feet now," he laughed. The cat did, but the fall was too great for him to jump up and scurry away as a cat would normally do.

***

Across town, an old abandoned warehouse sat secluded on

a street that people only drove through as a shortcut to somewhere else. The police would cruise by it about once every evening on their rounds just to make sure that it wasn't on fire or anything, but other than that, it remained invisible and forgotten. Victor had made that place his temporary home, a perfect place to hide. It gave him some shelter and a place to sleep at night.

One of the largest drawbacks of being an angel on the earth in human form was not having a place to live. Most of what Victor needed to survive on he found that old abandoned warehouse: a creaky, musty smelling cot, an old office chair to sit in, and a table. He had his own little room in the corner near a window that gave him a little light from one of the few street lamps that still worked or hadn't had its bulbs broken by kids. It wasn't much, but it was home.

A small gymnasium stood nearby. It had all the bathroom and shower facilities which he could use when able to get in there to use them. An integral part of the Watcher Angel training focused on survival techniques, which included care for a human body, such as bathing and other rituals for remaining... clean. In his short time as a human, Victor gained a new respect for the human plight.

He did more on that day than he had for many days before. Not knowing how his new form would react, he went about his day as if nothing differed. Anyone who has ever had an extreme injury knows it takes time to get back to par again. Victor did not know that. He halfway expected to jump right back into action, but quickly discovered the opposite. Not being used to the form, his actions took a great toll on him. By the time he made the three-mile walk back to the warehouse, he was ready to faint. Far into the next day, he woke up to an ache in his neck and a strange rumbling sensation in his stomach.

"All of this... humanity," he grumbled as he got himself ready to go to the gym. He had inquired about a job, cleaning and such, or whatever they needed for him to do. He just needed it for the next few weeks. The lady that he had talked to told him to come back early in the morning and talk to the owner.

Victor had two problems facing him as he walked to the gym. Hunger, and he did not know the time. *Time,* he thought as he limped along without his cane. *There is no training that could fully prepare anyone for this.* By the end of the day, he would fully know how slow time seems to pass when one has nothing to do.

Victor told the man at the gym a sob story, all true, about his circumstances. He needed a shower and bathroom facilities. In exchange for the use of the facilities and a tiny daily sum, he offered to work for him a few hours a day doing anything that he wished for him to do. The manager took pity on him and agreed to give him a job.

He was to work there several hours per day cleaning, cutting grass, weeding, sweeping, stacking weights, washing towels, and the list went on, and the manager agreed to give him a small bit of money each afternoon so that he could eat and buy a few supplies.

After a few days, he gave Victor a key so that he could get in whenever he needed to. The man always locked up the valuables and took the money with him. He didn't see the problem with Victor having the keys, and he trusted Victor.

"Something may happen and you may need a shower or have an emergency... uh, need." Ron, the owner of the gym, quipped and chuckled. Victor returned the laugh in agreement.

The man opened his trust to Victor, and Victor swore not to breach that trust. "The first sign of trouble," he warned, "and you're out of here."

The owner was a good man, with a big heart, a deacon at one of the smaller churches in town. He'd always had a soft spot in his heart for people who were down on their luck and needed some help. *And this poor soul*, he thought as he watched Victor trying his best to work with one arm, busted ribs and a limp, *definitely needs some help.*

Ron trusted the young man, and felt that although he gave his normal stern warning that it was not at all warranted. After several days of his hard work and good nature, Victor proved the man's trust to be justified, and the two of them became fast, good friends.

Victor stayed away from Tiffany for a time, partly from the confusion of the sudden influx of powerful emotions that he didn't understand. He also needed to take the time to heal. He didn't want to chance another incident like the one on the porch before, although that embrace and soft kiss remained in his mind; his dreams. He needed some time to sort things through in his mind before he made rash decisions through human emotion instead of angelic wisdom. Since he didn't trust his ability to refrain from, or even understand, his emotions, he thought it would be safer for him to stay away until he figured everything out.

At first he worked an hour here and there, and when he got tired, he sat down and rested, or quit for the day. As time went on, he worked more. Ron didn't mind that Victor worked slowly at first, and understood. After about a week, Victor walked without a limp and had tossed the sling. Much of his strength had returned to him. After another hard week of work, the owner of the gym gave him the day off. Victor broke his fast and visited Tiffany.

The night before he went to see her, a strange, yet not surprising, visitor came to see Victor.

Chapter Four

After his strange "thought monologue," one that is stereotypical of the hackneyed villain of the story, on the night that Victor last visited Tiffany, Jason left his roost and follow Victor home. Victor hadn't made it far, limping along, even with the time wasted by Jason in his plotting and cat flicking. Envious rage filled his essence and Jason wanted to kill both Tiffany and Victor, and since Victor was wide open to attack now, he formulated his plan and plotted the moment to strike.

Then, he thought, *when I have Victor at my mercy, I will take Tiffany.* Jason, still quite drawn to her and rather taken by her charms and those *wonderfully entrancing eyes*, felt bewitched by her beauty. He hated feeling in such a way. Twisted. Confused. Tortured.

Those eyes! He thought, *it's always those eyes. They bore into you like molten steel.* He could always see them staring at him, glistening, fearless and always in control. He swore to put fear into those eyes once again; fear and pain. Then, before he took her life, he would pluck them out of her skull. His eyes reddened with the thought, *but first,* he continued as he followed Victor to his abandoned abode. *I must eliminate her Watcher. Now that he is human, it will be easy.*

Jason watched from the rafters in Victor's home as Victor slept for a long period. Jason seized the opportunity to explore the warehouse and by the time that Victor woke up, Jason's plan was already in place, and his trap set. But he must bide his time and spring his trap at the best possible moment. Otherwise, it would all be for naught.

Since he didn't know when that would be, he used his free time to torment Tiffany. He would not put his plan into action until Victor returned. *Patience,* he hissed. Over the next couple of weeks, he went back to the warehouse several times to ensure that no one had discovered or disturbed his trap. One evening, Victor saw him as he left.

———

Victor recognized Jason in his true ghoulish form and it shocked him because he never thought that he would see him again. *I should have known better.* This prompted him to protect Tiffany, even if it meant giving his life. He was always willing to die for her. This might be his chance.

———

While Victor had been working and healing, Jason composed a symphony of torment for Tiffany. After taking Victor down, Jason planned for it to lead to her pain and end in her death, which would be the crescendo for his aria of evil. He had to get rid of those eyes that cast such a spell on him. It was all that occupied his thoughts and as he again sat upon his perch up in the tree outside of Tiffany's bedroom window, mumbling to himself.

With the fire in his eyes, he stared as the evil plot unfolded in his mind, piece by piece. He reared his head back and laughed wickedly, transitioning to a lusty howl of screeching, eerie pain. Tiffany, who had just turned out her light, peeked through the curtain to see what was making such an awful noise. Somehow, she knew, and the thought of it drove trepidation into her.

She whipped the curtain closed again. A motion that Jason did not miss. He gave an evil sneer while glaring at the window, and whispered in his demonic tone, "Yes, my dear. Soon, your Victor will be dead and you, my pretty with the piercing blue eyes, will be my toy. With no Watcher, you will be my pet to do with as I please."

***

Uncanny noises that echoed in the night outside brought Tiffany to her window. At first, she tried not to look, but curiosity won out. Not seeing anything, yet knowing what darkened in the night, she snapped the curtain closed, but it didn't curtail the unsettling feeling that encompassed her spirit on that evening.

She tried to push the thoughts of what might happen outside of her window away as she prayed, "Dear Jesus, please protect me in this night from whatever is out there that can hurt me." Shaking off her suspicions and refusing to believe what she thought to be true, she continued with the rest of her prayer. If she had learned anything from that experience, it was to never forget to say her prayers.

After praying, she felt a better, but still couldn't shake the awful feeling that someone or something terrible lurked just outside. She tried to shrug it off as just being paranoid as she had many nights before, but the fear just wouldn't leave her be. *I can't go through life jumping at every strange sound in the night.* She told herself, *it's just some dog howling at the moon.* It was a good attempt.

Sometimes in her younger years when she would be afraid of some movie that she watched, a limb scratching the window, or anything that would scare a little girl in the darkness, her daddy would come and console her. He made things better for a little while, but as soon as he left, the scary thoughts would return. Then, after she prayed her nightly prayers, she would feel alright. What she didn't know was that while she was praying and afraid, Victor worked against the forces of darkness that tried to drive fear into her soul. God is all powerful and with a thought, could eliminate the problem. He would often let the Watcher do whatever he could first.

Although she felt the peace and comfort from the Holy Spirit, the type of peace that will eliminate fear, something amiss on that night. A feeling she couldn't figure it out, or at least, she couldn't let herself admit what she suspected. She knew she would be safe, but something that she just couldn't, or wouldn't, allow herself to put her finger on caused her alarm.

***

Jason attempted nothing that night to strike fear into Tiffany, aside from his piercing howl, but he sat on his limb and stare lustfully at the window all night, anticipating the moment that he would make his move. He stirred ominous sounds in the night, moved the tree limbs to cast strange shadows into her room, but this was all in his patient preparation for the moment that his evil plan would unfold. He laughed again, leading to the same guttural howl as before, and smiled when he finished, knowing that he had once again awoken his prey. Drool oozed from the corners of his elongated mouth as his lust grew with his malevolent grin.

One night he stepped up his plan a bit more by appearing outside of Tiffany's window as a ghostly apparition, moaning and screaming. He could feel her fear as it arose within her; a supple snack to feed his desires. More and more she prayed, and less and less she felt the comforting of the Spirit of God. Jason knew she weakened with each haunting, and soon he would capture her and feed off of her fear and destroy her soul.

***

During the weeks Victor worked at the gym, allowing some of his wounds to heal while slowly gaining his strength, Tiffany came out of the school every afternoon and wonder why Victor had not come. Every day she walked home and felt empty and alone. Each night, before her tormenter showed up, she would begin for him by tormenting herself. She wondered what had happened to the familiar stranger that walked her home that afternoon and spilled his heart to her, only to disappear into the night. Was he being honest that night, or had she latched onto another lunatic bent on hurting her? For all she knew, he may have been the one who was outside of her window each night as a ghostly apparition or making awful sounds in the night, testing her resolve, her faith, and overwhelming her heart with fear.

Somehow, though, she knew it wasn't him out there, but someone or something else, someone familiar. But she didn't want to allow her thoughts to go there. However, she trusted Victor. Although she had just met him, she felt as if she had known him for her entire life; like he had been there, watching. Yet now she felt so alone. Her lonely pain would turn to tears, and she would remember laying her head upon the shoulder of her protector, nuzzling her face against his neck, and in that moment, feeling safer than she had ever felt before. She could feel his love for her and how reassuring to feel loved in such a way, especially *when I love him too;* the revelation did not come as complete shock to her. Somehow, she had always known.

With a strange note of irony, her love was that same unrequited love that he had spoken to her about a few days before. She longed for the embrace of one that she should have never met, that feeling of being loved in such a pure, unadulterated way. In the loneliness of those nights, she understood what he meant by the perfect love that he had for her. She knew she had somehow grown to love him in the same way. But, now that she realized and understood everything, he wasn't there, and it left her to wonder.

"Victor?" she called out into the open air. No response. Had they sent him to her for only one day, that one moment in time? Had they had forced him to leave her because he crossed some line in telling her the truth? She longed for the embrace of the one she never should have had to begin with. All she could do was hold on to the memory of that one evening with a boy that she never knew but knew too well; a boy who knew her better than anyone except God.

The days passed, and each day Tiffany walked home alone. At least she thought she was alone. Her temporary Watcher followed her every day, but so did her tormentor. He stalked her every move from the shadows, visible yet never to be seen. He was everywhere, and he noticed her loneliness each day and relished in her pain. The more anguish he could force upon her, the better, because she was... *too pure, too nice, too innocent and had too much life... I must feed on that life.* He swore to take the life from her eyes and the smile from her face. Although he thought someone had already taken the smile, at least for the moment.

Finally, one afternoon when Tiffany peered across the street in aimless hope, she saw the one who she had been thinking and even dreaming of, the one who forced love into her, although a small portion had just leaked from him into her. Her smile returned. Victor had healed a lot and rather quickly, or so she thought.

He no longer had the cane or the sling for his arm. The casts were still on his forearm and leg, and he was still tender around the ribs. She found this out when she ran across the street to embrace him, and if her vice-grip of a hug wasn't enough, when she pulled back, her smile disappeared and she smacked his side. "Where have you been? I have been through… it's been awful…" She couldn't find the right words and stopped talking as he winced in pain. "What's the matter? Oh," she covered her mouth and smiled while apologizing with her gaze, "I'm so sorry, I forgot about your ribs." She then dropped her smile and bore her eyes into his.

At that moment, Victor forgot his pain and the world around him. She then hugged him softly, laying her head on his chest. He breathed a deep sigh of relief as she held him and he returned her soft embrace. Pulling her head back, their eyes locked again. Then, as natural and unconscious as anything could be, Victor bent down and gave her a kiss. He felt like he could dance on the head of a needle. When they released, she again laid her head on his chest, listening to the beat of his heart and the smooth flow of his steady breathing. It soothed her.

After a moment, she let go, although not wanting to. She stepped back and looked deep into his eyes, and smiled as she saw a tear rolling down his cheek. She thought she understood, but truly she did not. No one could have understood unless they too were like Victor, a lifelong victim of unrequited love only to realize that their dream had finally come true. If they could have, they would have stood there, locked in their embrace forever.

Chapter Five

Earlier that day, Victor rose at dawn and unbeknownst to him, he would become the victim of the longest day of his seventeen years upon the earth. Nothing in heaven had prepared him for the slow decay of time when he looked forward to something. He had heard that a watched pot never boiled, but never understood the meaning. Ten minutes is ten minutes either way. Then he realized that something happened to one's perspective when anticipation adds to the conundrum. He had heard humans refer to watching paint dry, or the grass grow, or the hair growing on a horse. He never knew the true meaning, until that day.

He had the day off, the first full day off he had in over a week. He intended to meet Tiffany after school that day and again walk her home. As the day began with the daily requirements of care for his human form, Victor set out to stand across the street from the school and wait for Tiffany. He soon realized that he had very little concept of time and the slow progress of it as one waited. Patience, a concept that essentially deals with time, was not a lesson Victor learned well.

In eternity, life continues without limitations. In heaven, nothing ends; beginnings, yes, many beginnings, but never endings. This concept proves as difficult to grasp for angels as the concept of forever is for humanity. Humanity can imagine what eternity may be, but nothing exists in our experiences to compare the hypothesis.

At the Academy, Einstein did a superb job getting the Angels to understand it, but nothing or no one, even Einstein, could teach the concept of the passing of time better than living in it.

The sun rises, gets hotter as the day proceeds and cooler as it sets, and then the darkness comes and without sleep, it never seems to end.

The idea came to Victor as he watched the sun rise to its peak and then transcend again to include a field trip to earth during the time training. A field trip designed to teach the passing of time. Let the Angels in training spend a day doing nothing but watching the sunrise and staying in the same place until it sets. This is contingent upon one's perspective, for the sun stays in one place and the earth moves around it. After the sun sets, the group should remain there and wait until the sun rises again. A day by human standards and would torture any angel and that is how Victor felt, tortured. It was like watching the grass grow, waiting for Tiffany.

After a lifetime, as it seemed to Victor, the bell rang across the street, but Victor hadn't noticed it. He had been peeling his thousandth blade of grass when it rang.

Earlier in the day, when he had heard the bell to change classes, he jumped with excitement and his heart leaped. When nobody came out and no guard stood at the crosswalk to usher the walkers across the street, he sat back down with a huff and a sigh. This happened several times, and the last time, the one time that he should have been ready, he ignored it.

As he reached for another blade of grass to peel, he saw students heading for the parking lot. The police officer acting as a crossing guard had appeared to direct traffic. His heart skipped with excitement while a knot formed in his stomach; his breathing grew shallow. A smile plastered itself onto his face, and he couldn't contain himself when he saw Tiffany coming toward the street to make her way across. Feeling his heart pound, he stared, dumbstruck.

When Tiffany saw Victor across the street, she gave a huge smile and her eyes gleamed, her heart also skipped a beat with excitement, but as she walked across the street, the smile faded into a scowl by the time she stood in front of Victor. His smile had also faded, replaced with a look of utter confusion. Before he could ask, "What is it?" she answered his question with a smack on his arm.

"Where have you been? It's been over a week." Victor stood speechless, trying to think of what he could say. Not thinking of anything useful. He shrugged, and his mouth hung open. Just like any regular male of the human species in such a situation.

He stood for a moment with his mouth hanging open accompanied by a fixed, blank stare as his arms pointed in each direction at his side, keeping his shoulders shrugged. Unlike other boys his *age*, Victor had no clue where he had been for the last couple of weeks. At least not with ease of explanation.

As Victor scrambled to think of anything to say in response, Tiffany's frown and scowl turned to sudden relief, and she wrapped her arms around him and squeezed. Slowly, as the shock and confusion abated, Victor lowered his arms and returned to her embrace. Her grip was painful to his bruised ribs, but he didn't care.

After a moment, she raised her head. Still locked in the embrace, she looked him in the eye. That's when the overwhelming urge to kiss her came over him. So he did. She caught in shock her breath and tried to recover from such a raw, passionate kiss and then said, eyes squinting in a demanding fashion and lightly nudging him away. "Don't you ever do that to me again!"

Still a bit confused, Victor gave a small but perplexed smile and nodded as he let her go. "I mean, staying away for so long," she smiled, still aloof, "not the kiss. That was fine." Victor blushed and then he walked her home.

As they walked, he told her about his job at the gym. How the man there was so nice to take care of him. He talked about people entertaining angels unaware and how the man who owned the gymnasium will receive a special blessing from the Lord for being so nice to him. He knew he could talk freely to Tiffany, even if he shouldn't have been. If he could see the scowl on Raul's face, or if he even knew that Raul had been with him since he took human form to recover from his injuries, he would not have continued to talk in such a manner.

Tiffany was a good listener, as well as a kind, beautiful face to speak to. She knew how Victor felt about her, for Victor had not been secretive about that since he let her know of his true origins. She didn't mind that either, for she had grown quite taken by him as well. Between their last meeting and now, she thought of little more than her angel and his unrequited love. The more time they spent together, the stronger their bond became. It was a sweet story for any who may have been privy to notice, but a recipe for disaster.

During the afternoon and on into that evening, the two of them stayed out on the stoop and talked about everything they could think of. They enjoyed the peace of the cool afternoon. Neither of them thought of the world outside of the porch.

They laughed together until they cried. Then their conversation grew so serious, one would think that they would never laugh again. The cycle would start all over again. The sweet aroma of their budding love could intoxicate anyone who may have happened by. It was a dream-come-true for Victor. He could finally share the love that he bottled up for so long. Victor wished the day *would* last forever. But, as it is with time, All Things Must Pass.

***

Lurking in the shadows was someone that oozed unhappiness, and he brooded over the display of love on the porch. It made him want to projectile vomit. Wherever you found Tiffany, Jason was never far away, waiting and plotting his revenge. Revenge for what? For being alive. He could almost taste the victory of taking her life from her. He would have his sacrifice. Even if it was the last thing he ever did.

Perched on his limb like an old crow in the dark, he glared at the stoop where Victor and Tiffany sat. He couldn't hear what they were talking about, but the love that floated up from there churned his stomach. *Love.* He winced and tried to shake it off, as if it were some sort of filth. *What a weak and sick emotion.* Then he sneered and said, "But, God is love. Bah. He didn't love me." Satan fooled him and all into believing that God never loved them. Being so separated from God removed all love from them. They may have known it once, but no more.

———

Jason waited with bated breath for the perfect moment to strike. He had an evil grin plastered to his face as he thought about how his plan rolled into motion and everything would end soon, even that brief love affair of theirs. All he had to do was spring the trap. He could almost smell the death and taste the victory. *Oh yes,* he inhaled the essence of his lust, rolling his eyes in ecstasy. *I can hear her scream.*

Little do they know, he continued with his smirk and yearning stare at his two mortal enemies as they spent the evening on the carport talking and laughing *that they are playing right into my trap. Soon,* he thought, *I'll give the two of you a little more time to get even closer and then...* he clapped his hands together. Friction tossed sparks from his gnarled fingers, and then he tilted his head back and laughed. An evil shrill filled the air.

While he waited for the perfect time, he sat on his limb, and each night when Tiffany lay alone in her bed, he would do everything within his power to haunt her and drive fear into her heart. Of course, she would run to Victor for help, and would soon tell him what had been happening. The saddest part of it all, the most appealing to Jason, was that Victor could do nothing about it.

Chapter Six

Tiffany and Victor grew closer and closer as time passed. Victor lived a dream, but a significant problem presented itself, one that he had not wished to think about. He had been waiting for this moment his entire life. Now he realized that his time as a human on the earth drew short. Soon his wounds would heal, and when that happened, he would return to his former duties, being a Watcher Angel. He hoped to be with Tiffany, but she would not know that he existed. Soon, with the passing of time, Victor feared she would forget. Oh, he would remain a distant memory, but as time grew with him remaining unseen, she would move on. He would again know the torture of unrequited love.

Later that evening at the warehouse, these thoughts haunted him, and he allowed himself to face the inevitable. He arrived at a common human decision before he drifted into sleep, to take one day at a time. Fretting would solve nothing; never has. He would enjoy humanity, his time with Tiffany and all the benefits that came with that time for as long as he could. He would worry about having to leave later.

Before he slept, he decided tomorrow he would go to Tiffany's carport again. He vowed within himself to never avoid her again. The meeting was fabulous.

As the days and evenings passed with delight and increasing compassion, the spark between the two youngsters grew. Beautiful days seemed to never end, yet flew by too fast. Victor could live like this forever. Yet he struggled with what to do. Then one day, after much thought and torture, Victor decided and he revealed that decision to Tiffany.

"I'm not going back," he spat out. Interrupting a peaceful silence. He said it as if he hadn't said it right then, he never would have been brave enough to say it.

"Huh?" Tiffany replied, "I'm confused." She thought, "Go back where?"

"To being an angel, your Watcher," he said, still prattling, as he couldn't hold the words back. He allowed them to leap from his mind and through his mouth.

***

Raul stood in shock, staring at Victor with his mouth gaping. He didn't know what to think. Victor couldn't see him, but if he could smack some sense into him somehow, he would. His reaction mirrored that of Victor's when Tiffany had first been so intent on telling her lie. He had to stop Victor from making such a foolish mistake. *Victor is speaking and thinking with human emotions*, Raul thought. He had to find some way to get Victor to think like an angel again. How? Raul rummaged through his mind for a solution, but none was found.

With all his experience, training, and expertise, nothing prepared him for what he had just witnessed. Victor, if even temporarily, was a human, and he had free will. His choice must be honored. Raul hoped that Victor's choices would not separate him from God or cause him to bring harm to himself. As his Watcher, Raul could do nothing to stop him. *If I could only talk to him, show him the foolishness of this decision...* He knew he couldn't do that anymore. Such is the life of a watcher.

***

Victor continued with his revelation to Tiffany.

"I can stay with you and live the rest of my life as a human." He smiled and drew in a deep, shuttered breath with excitement. "All I have to do is choose to remain human and I can stay. Then we can..."

"Whoa, slow down there, big boy." She held up her hand, backing up a bit. "Don't you think this is sudden. Haven't you thought about what I would think? I love you and all, but..." she stopped, not finding the right words. Victor's excitement and smile faded as she continued, "… but I barely know you. I know you have been here my whole life. That is the coolest thing I have ever known. You know me better than I know myself, yet, I know nothing about you. I can't even remember you from when you saved me all those years ago."

She paused again, this time much longer, hoping it would sink in. She searched his eyes, looking from one to the other. They both said the same thing. This crushed Victor, and it shattered Tiffany, but she knew she needed to continue.

Placing her hand on the side of his face, she continued studying his eyes. She drew as close as she could without touching noses and finished her thought, "I know you don't understand because you haven't been," she swallowed at the strangeness of the next word, "human for long and don't know many others besides me, but I have a life. I'm only sixteen and I have a lot of life to live. I don't even know what I'm going to do after high school. My life is an open book, yet to be written and you…" she smiled, "you have a greater duty than I can ever imagine. All I am saying is don't be hasty. I can't live with you giving up heaven for me. Although, it is the sweetest and most romantic thing I have ever heard. One Man did that for me already, and I hate he had to. Think it through. Give me some time. Don't make the choice now. Wait until you are absolutely sure. If you aren't… well, what if something happens to me; to us? What then? You remain here until you die, living in the misery of being human? Alone." She shook her head and somehow her eyes did not leave his. "I love you, Victor, but you have a greater purpose, a greater existence. As romantic as all this is," she laughed, a lovely smile that melted Victor's heart, "you can't give that up for me."

Tiffany in her wisdom gave Victor some points that he had never considered, and he was quite ashamed that he had been so hasty. The amount of superior wisdom came from Tiffany impressed Raul. There was indeed much more to this human than her beautiful exterior. Most humans didn't impress Raul much he was the Watcher of Jesus Christ and compared to Him every other human just couldn't compare, but Tiffany showed great caliber. He now understood why Victor was so taken by her. It went deeper than his duty of love for her, an almost forbidden love, but for the first time, Raul understood it. He bore witness to her magnificence.

Without pause or apology, Tiffany did what Raul failed to do. She talked some sense into Victor, who acted purely on human emotions.

That night Victor slept little. Neither did Tiffany, but for different reasons. Victor couldn't stop thinking about the possibilities that were before him. In a matter of just a few weeks as a human, he had gone from angel and stoic philosopher, proud of his tradition and heritage, to riding the human rollercoaster of confusion and emotion. Was he really willing to give up his heritage? His dilemma heightened. He had gone from an angel with unrequited love for the young lady that he watched over, which is not so unusual, to a former angel in a human body stricken by forbidden love. Should he give it all up for the hopes that he would spend a life of love as human, or should he return to having love, yet having to swallow the pain of having it unreturned?

As a Watcher, love was a mandate. To act upon any love in a manner was unthinkable. Angels have been injured in the past and had to take human form. Although some fell into the trap of emotionalism and some had fallen into the fascination of the beauty of another, none had ever fallen so deeply in love. This presented a greater problem; one so great that even Raul railed with no solution. Tiffany had done well in bringing reality to the mind of Victor, but Victor could not deny his feelings, although unthinkable and almost forbidden, or at least unspeakable. Love is the greatest of all emotions. It can drive someone back to God, but the love of forbidden fruit can drive them farther away. Although at the moment, this love that Victor held remained innocent, it could quickly escalate into something far more carnal. Raul felt relieved as Tiffany remained strong and held great moral standards.

Although Tiffany had talked a small of sense into Victor, Raul was still unsure of Victor's intentions. Raul knew of Victor's love for Tiffany. He and Victor had discussed it frequently. When Victor drifted to sleep, Raul went to speak with the angels.

***

In the meantime, Tiffany lay in her bed wide awake and thinking on similar matters. She knew Victor loved her, and that he took advantage of his time as a human to show her his love. The worst part rested because she loved him back, even as odd as it all may have seemed. He opened his heart to her, unlike any other person she had ever known, and she drew closer to him than to any other young boy or man that she had ever known. But was any of this even right?

It had to be wrong to love an angel in this manner, even in human form. The age difference alone, *huh*, she thought with a nervous laugh. *Who knows how old he could be? He could be thousands of years old. And what if we grew together, stay together and got married? What about kids? Would we have them? Would they be some sort of mix between human and angel*? The thought was terrifying. These things needed to be thought through and discussed.

After Tiffany lay down to think, the haunting returned. Outside of her window, Jason stood, waiting to torment her for yet another night. Brainwashing. Instilling fear. Parlor tricks with flashing lights, smoke, and mirrors. If he could have gotten close enough, he would have slipped her mind-altering drugs. Sorcery.

As part of his sorcerer's ways over the years, he got people hooked on drugs. In doing that, he held the ultimate control and power over them. People would often do anything that he asked for their next fix or high. Soon, the drugs wouldn't get them high, but they need the drugs to sustain life. To his chagrin, Jason could not get close enough to Tiffany. So, he resorted to cheap theatrics instead.

He used the old stereotypical haunting from the old ghost stories; dragging chains in the attic, moaning apparitions in the dark corners, wicked demonic images, writings on the walls, taps on the windows and all the other stuff that demon ghouls often used to torment their prey.

Many believe in ghosts, but they do not exist. Demons always do hauntings. Yes, they are spirits, but they are not ghosts. Demons could and would pose as a member of someone's deceased family to *speak to them from beyond the grave*; just another tactic of trying to control the minds of superstitious human beings. Often, the most superstitious are those most susceptible to attack.

Although tortured and afraid, Tiffany did all that she could do to ignore the hauntings. She didn't know who tortured her, or why. She had her suspicions. Since escaping the cabin, she expected the members of the cult to come. This should have made her paranoid, but all it did was increase her faith. Not knowing what else to do, she asked the Lord for help. In this last resort lies the greater solution.

Most would give in, but she asked God to speak to her, to whisper peace into her heart amid chaos that surrounded her. She would put on her headphones, tuning out the surroundings as she prayed, and fall asleep in the arms of the Lord. She knew he would let nothing happen to her. If Victor could have seen her, he would have beamed with pride. None of it would have happened if Victor were there, but God made Tiffany of sturdy stuff.

The faith and poise of this sturdy young lady was incomparable among her peers, and she would not let such things as a fake haunting bother her. She knew ghosts didn't exist, just demons posing as them. The Lord was there, so she had no reason to fear. Although she kept telling herself these things and tried to stay strong, after a time under constant attack, even the strongest wall would break. That is why Jason would never give up.

Chapter Seven

Raul stood with the archangels of heaven, Michael and Gabriel. They walked in the garden, a favorite pastime in the eternal world of the first heaven. This world of the angels, the grand creation of God, would take the breath away from the greatest of artists and baffle their imaginations.

Waterfalls of many colors, lush green hillsides with mighty rock face cliffs beneath them. The waterfalls would drop for miles, emptying into a vast ocean of fresh, drinkable water. All anyone had to do to get a refreshing dose of heaven's water was go to any stream, lake, river or ocean, cup their hands and take a drink. Beautiful and perfect fruit trees stood everywhere, asking for those who walked by to stop and enjoy the supple fruit that always adorned them. One season occupied this heaven. The same temperate climate remained and never a shade of darkness or a corner for anything to lurk or hide. No one had to worry about sweat, or flies, no cold or rain; the perfect place of perfect peace and splendor.

Raul had been exiled to earth or to the Watcher Academy, which prepared angels for earth. The academy had its own sense of heavenly beauty and peace. He forgot how he missed the old heaven, the first place that God ever created. He sighed and then inhaled deep through his nose, taking in the perfectly fragrant air.

"Miss it, don't you?" Gabriel asked. He plucked a perfect, untainted flower from the gardens and brought it to his nose, using all of his senses to enjoy its flawlessness. Raul followed in the same pattern, while Michael walked on by with his arms crossed behind his back. The others caught up. "Huh," Gabriel continued as they caught up to the fast-walking Michael, "it all brings to mind the greatest mystery of all eternity past, present and future." He shook his head and frowned. "Why Lucifer would ever give up all of this excellence to live on the imperfect and ever-increasing filth of the earth, boggles the mind. He confessed and make things right. Jehovah Lord gave him that chance, but as the wise man of earth once said and I paraphrase, 'pride comes before every fall,' this holds true of Lucifer and those who followed him on his foolish quest."

"Indeed," Raul raised the flower taking in the perfect beauty and closed his eyes in ecstasy. He knew well how nasty earth could be. Even the training academy seemed more like heaven compared to earth. He loved the place, but often wondered why human beings fought so hard to stay alive on earth when they could live in such a place of eternal tranquility. If they only knew what awaited them by choosing God's gift, they would never live as they do.

"So," Michael interrupted, "why have you come, old friend? What was so urgent that you needed to speak without waiting?"

"It's Victor. He is about to decide. I don't know how to handle the situation. As far as I know, outside of the fallen, this hasn't been an issue." Raul stared at the wise archangel, waiting for his response. Gabriel stared at him, waiting his turn for input.

"Ah, Victor," Michael lowered his head and shook it, "yes, a bit troubled he has been. I imagine he faces quite the dilemma." Raul squinted in question at him. This did not go unnoticed. "Oh, I know," Michael continued not wanting to offend his old friend by debasing his favorite pupil, "he has meant well with all that he has done and has done more than an adequate job, but this deep love that he holds for his human is causing him much grief. He has allowed himself to grow too close."

"It's never wrong to love too much, master," Raul responded, "and as for his willingness to give his life for Tiffany, that is an unwritten part of the mandate of the Watcher Angels. We are to protect them even to the death."

Michael waved his hand at him and then returned it to the

former position behind his back and continued to walk. "Yes, I had forgotten the attachment all Watchers take for a moment and I also realize that we expected you to do everything within the power given to you to keep them safe and from falling away from Father."

Gabriel spoke up as Michael stopped. "What has he done that gave the Master of Watcher Angels pause in such a way? What could cause you of all angels to question?" He stared at Raul, awaiting his response.

"He," Raul sighed as if he were searching for the right words, "he wishes to remain human and live out his life. He has gotten a taste of humanity as he heals from his vast injuries, and I'm afraid the human emotions of that form are clouding his judgment."

The three angels stopped. The two archangels looked at Raul with surprise, but the shock soon disappeared from their faces. Gabriel turned his gaze to Michael. "I suppose we should have seen this one coming, brother. Ever since he developed an extra-special attraction with the special soul of this young lady, the possibility remained that his love would grow this way."

"Yes," Michael nodded, "indeed his love for her has always been strong, but has faith, my brother. Maybe it will prevail in the end in bringing him to his senses. As soon as the demons discover that an angel who has given up his powers, their torture of him will never cease. What they will put the young lady through... I shudder to think of such things. We will have to pray that his love will reveal the genuine spirit of his duty to Tiffany."

"But what shall I do, master?" Raul questioned, still seeking aid for his problem.

"There is nothing that to do, Master Watcher, except let him choose. He is human at the moment and falls under free will." Raul had stopped, but Michael continued to walk as he talked.

"If he chooses humanity, then I will stay with him as his watcher to protect him from the demons that will come after him." Michael stopped and turned his attention to Raul again. Gabriel was now at his side.

"Then you must do what you must. Keep in mind if he chooses humanity, Tiffany will need a new watcher, and may be without one for a time. Are you willing to watch over them both, as you have been?" Michael stared.

Raul thought for a moment. Michael brought up something he hadn't thought of before. What would happen to Tiffany if Victor remained human? Who would watch over and protect her? Raul has performed double duty before, but for only a short period. Could he do so for the rest of their lives? "As you said, Master, I must do as I must."

Michael smiled, "I suppose you must, and I can see no one better fit for the job than the great Master Watcher, Raul." He turned to finish his walk through the garden, arms still at post behind his back, "Go with God, my friend. We will see you when you need us again, or when we see you. We will meditate on this and discuss it further. If a solution arises, we will act or instruct you on how to act." With that, the archangels walked away. Raul returned to earth, knowing little more than he did before he came.

Chapter Eight

An unexpected visitor appeared in Victor's old abandoned warehouse; a visitor that hadn't been upon the earth for many generations. He often came in times past to warn people of things and give them some information that they needed to perform a task for God. Raul was around for many of these visits on his first assignment as a Watcher Angel. He never delivered information, for he was not a messenger, and he didn't receive any messages. He knew the information.

The last time the Archangel Gabriel came to earth, he warned Joseph in a dream to flee to Egypt before the slaughter of the innocents in Bethlehem. Raul remembered that gruesome night as if it just happened, and he always appreciated Gabriel for his warnings. Perhaps that was why he always held Gabriel in such high esteem. Michael had great attributes and Raul loved and respected him, just not as much as he did Gabriel.

For over two thousand years, neither Gabriel nor Michael entered the atmosphere of the earth. Now the silence would end as Gabriel came to visit Victor in a dream.

***

Earlier. After Raul left heaven to return to earth and watch over Victor, Michael and Gabriel discussed the situation further as they continued their stroll through the garden. Not to their complete surprise, Christ joined them who, of course, knew everything that had transpired, including their conversation with Raul. "A messenger must visit him," He advised.

"Cannot Raul tell him what he must do?" Michael replied.

"Raul cannot influence his free will and he cannot warn him directly. No," he sighed, "one of you must warn him in a dream that if he persists in this decision of his that he and young Tiffany will perish. The Father has grand plans for her and her family, a powerful family it will be, so she must not die. If Victor persists in this choice, then she will die. If she dies, monumental works for the Kingdom will never begin."

Gabriel nodded, "I will go." He smiled at Christ while placing a hand on Michael's shoulder, "I think he fears you too much brother, no offence."

Jesus smiled at this playful banter between brothers and nodded to Gabriel in thanks. And as He arrived, He disappeared. "Well," Gabriel smiled, patted Michael on the shoulder again, and sighed, "I have a trip to earth to plan. Huh," he nodded, looking at the flowers, "didn't think I'd be back there before The Great Battle in the end."

"Gabriel," Michael called to him as he started away. Gabriel stopped and turned his attention to him. "Father Speed on your journey. The wastes of the earth should not be taken lightly. Take care of where you go. The demons know their time is short and prepare for the end. If they were to find you there..." he shook his head and sighed. "It is a much worse place than it was the last time that you went." Then he looked at the flowers. "As soon as you, the archangel Gabriel, arrive, they will all know. Word travels fast amongst the angels and demons."

"Yes, brother," Gabriel smiled again. "I will go prepared and armed. Thank you for your wisdom and concern." Gabriel turned, as did Michael, folding his hands behind his back. He stared at the waterfall that seemed to flow into the nothingness,the mists on the horizon. Awe-inspiring beauty. The freshness of the air. The sweet aroma and the Joy in the Love of God.

"Such a beautiful place where we angels live." Michael sighed again. "God be with you, my brother. You now return to the closest thing to hell as we have ever seen. Compared to this place, earth is hell. Why would Lucifer's angels, give up so much to gain so little?"

Chapter Nine

Michael was right, Gabriel thought with a sigh of shock as he arrived. *What a dreadful place earth has become. What have they done to it?* Compared to where he had been for the past two thousand years, even the most beautiful place on earth seemed but a desert wasteland. Many places of beauty could compare to the heavens, but mostly earth was barren, dirty, and covered with human waste and inventions. Clutter.

They gather in centers of commerce and crawl over of top one another like ants on a hill. With all the open space in the world, it baffled him why they would choose to pile on top of each other. Then murder, rape, pillage, steal, and hate each other for their differences. Gabriel and all the angels understood this the least. *What differences? They are all human, no matter what language they speak, where they came from or the color of their skin.*

Gabriel wished he could force them to understand, to face the truth, show them they were all the same. Without the savior, Christ, they would perish. He had to remind himself that the time for this revelation had not yet come. Gabriel would help during that time, but he would not rescue the lost. That job belonged to the Lord; in Christ alone would the world be saved.

He passed by a bum in the street, starving, drunk and dying, and it reminded him of the gruesome reality that is humanity and their freedom to choose. Taking a quick field trip to some places on the earth helped him to put things into perspective. He had heard the horror stories, but never had he seen such devastation and degradation in his entire existence. *It's a good thing I'm not God*, he thought, *because I would not save them.* Even he didn't have a complete grasp of the fullness of God's grace toward humanity and the complexity of His love. *And they don't even appreciate what God, what Christ has done for them. Most of them don't, anyway.*

After a few stops around the world to put things "into perspective", Gabriel reminded himself the reason for the trip. He joined Victor, who was for the time human. There were but two ways to communicate with him. To do so openly held the risk of being seen by others. The second method was through the indirect approach to dreams. The last choice held less danger of exposure, unless God willed for others to see. Gabriel planned to visit Victor in the night as he slept and give him a warning during his dream.

***

Jason loomed in the shadows over Victor's cot in his little corner of the abandoned warehouse, watching him sleep. His plan to trap Victor and take Tiffany drew close to fruition. Victor could revert to his formal Angelic glory now that all of his wounds had healed. But… If an accident were to befall him as a human, in his sleep, for example, then he could never revert to being an angel and Tiffany would belong to Jason. At least, that was Jason's plan.

He had already set the trap. Now he waited for the perfect moment to trigger it. His only regret: "I will be somewhere else when the plan goes down on Victor," he whispered. *When the plan goes down*, he laughed at himself. *I crack myself up.* He laughed again, almost out loud; *I just can't stop with these puns. Literally… when it all goes down.* His sinister grin broadened. Even now his form drew closer to the veritable monster that he was, and the longer he lingered, the less human he appeared. Of course, he didn't care anymore. Jason's mind was on one thing: the sweet taste of death, the deaths of Victor and Tiffany.

"Sleep, young human," he whispered behind a sneer, and his voice hissed like a snake's. "This is your last night on the earth. Look on the bright side." Jason's eyes lit up with the joy of his coming sarcasm. "at least they won't have to bury you. They will never find you. You will simply cease to exist to others." His voice changed to emphasize the sarcastic tone. "No, I'm afraid that you will everyone will forget you. I'm the only one who knows where you are, and I'm not telling a soul. Rest now, boy, who was once an angel... soon it will be as if you never were." Jason skulked away to find Tiffany and continue his plan to exact his vengeance upon her. Vengeance because she lived. Barring a miracle, Victor would not be there to save her. No one would.

***

Victor slept undisturbed. Gabriel stood over him, watching him sleep, wondering why any angel would choose such a frail existence, but he as a messenger didn't understand how God could even love most humans. Angels, he could understand. Humans were so... disobedient. God's love and grace are for all, no matter what. Angels didn't quite understand this. Only God could, truly. He gave grace to whoever asked for it and to the angels. God loves everyone.

Gabriel waved his hand over Victor, placing him in a deeper sleep so to incite a dream in him. Within seconds he could see Victor's eyes moving back and forth behind closed eyes. REM sleep. Taking a deep breath and closing his eyes to concentrate, for it had been quite a while since he had performed such a task, he began his work.

Gabriel had no problems getting through. Victor's mind remained untainted by human carnality, and the disease of sin had not yet taken hold of him. Although he held a great infatuation for one certain human being, none of the other human emotions of the carnal nature had entered him yet. If he remained human, then his mind would reach that realization one day, where he would have to make a choice between God and the world of sin. *Hopefully*, Gabriel thought, *we can stop that here tonight before it is too late.*

Entering Victor's dream, a fresh photograph that was only developing, Gabriel forged the vision that he wished Victor to see. He couldn't be too cryptic, for that would be left open to interpretation, and he couldn't be obvious either. Victor may not remember it. He had to form a dream farfetched, yet remain as simple as possible. After some thought, he had his plan and formed the dream in Victor's mind.

Victor dreamed of the cabin where Tiffany lay on the floor, tied up, surrounded by darkness with only the holes in the walls giving her light. Gabriel drew upon this image because it popped in the front of Victor's mind, and even in his waking moments it never traveled too far from his sub-consciousness. He blamed himself for allowing her to get into such a situation. The guilt from the image would not leave him. Gabriel capitalized on this.

In the dream, Victor stood at the door of the cabin, watching Tiffany squirm. Jason stood over her, laughing, with his knife drawn back, ready for the last thrust. Fear smothered Tiffany's essence, and she appeared defeated. Although he knew he had to stop what was happening, Victor couldn't draw himself any closer than where he stood in the doorway. This made Jason laugh all the more. Another villainous monologue that had become a part of his forte followed. Panic set in Victor's mind as he clamored to get to Tiffany, but no matter what he tried, he couldn't break free of whatever restrained him. In the human form, he could do nothing.

In a final desperate act to get to Tiffany, Victor became an angel again. As soon as he did this, he broke free of whatever bonds held him and got to Tiffany in time to save her.

He woke with a scream to lie in his cot at the warehouse. Gabriel stood next to him, and when Victor woke in such a manner, Gabriel opened his eyes. Victor saw him standing there. "Master?" He panted from the excitement and looked at Gabriel questionably. Without realizing it, he mimicked Tiffany with this look. "Gabriel?"

"Yes, Victor, it is I, the Archangel Gabriel. I have come to you with a message, so I sent you a dream." He waited before revealing what the dream should mean, because he wanted to hear Victor tell what it meant. Free will.

Victor looked down, deep in thought. "Yes." His eyes moved as he remembered the dream. "I see." He looked at Gabriel again with realization. "As a human, I couldn't save her, but as soon as I became an angel, I could. Does that mean that if I remain human, then I can't help her? She…" he gazed at the ground again. "She will die?" He furrowed his brow and looked away again. "Is she in trouble? Is that what you are telling me? I'm going to have to become an angel again to save her."

Gabriel nodded and then broke his silence. "If you remain human, then she will die, as will you."

"But every human dies." Victor replied.

"Yes, but in due season, and if you choose to remain human forever…" He shrugged.

"Wait," Victor interrupted, "how did you know I was going to give myself to Tiffany in the morning… oh," he realized, "never mind, Christ told you." Gabriel simply nodded. "Well then," Victor continued, looking away, "I have much to think about."

Think about?! Gabriel thought, exasperated. *What is there to think about? If you swear yourself to her and become human, then she will die and you with her.* He wanted to smack some sense into Victor. Gabriel could send a message and give guidance, but the choice still had to be Victor's.

Raul thought the same thing. He tried to see the dream and the conversation between Victor and Gabriel and he failed to notice the traps all around them. Just above them, in a hidden spot of the rafters, a timepiece flashing red numbers counted down. Several more in strategic places all around the warehouse also counted. Someone could have found them easily if they thought to look up. LOOK UP!

The foundation rocked around them as the timer counted down to zero and resulted in a powerful explosion. Several more exploded in brief sequence, ending with the one right above Victor's cot. The chain reaction resulted in collapsing walls and the ceiling cascaded, burying everything in sight. As the last bomb blew, Gabriel tossed himself over Victor, shielding him from the fallout and the explosion.

***

For the first time, Jason dared to enter Tiffany's room. For years he had longed to enter what he saw as an impenetrable fortress. As long as Victor lingered, it remained that way. Victor was not there. Tiffany was all alone. Jason had even kept her parents and brothers out of the way. No, he hadn't killed them, but they all would wake up with quite a headache.

Jason tormented and haunted her from a distance. This limited what he could do. With Victor gone, he felt he could do anything he wanted. He watched Tiffany sleep; she had such a peaceful beauty in rest. A small part of him enjoyed watching her sleep, but most of him longed to see pain and fear in her eyes.

After a moment or two of observing her at rest, he acted. The last time he abducted her, she went with him freely. This time it could prove difficult, for he would not trick her into coming along. He knew that he would have to force her. With the quickness of a striking rattlesnake, Jason grabbed Tiffany's ninety-five-pound frame, lifting her from the bed while covering her mouth to stifle the shrill scream that he knew she could give. As he ran out of the room and into the house she kicked and screamed and scrapped with him, but she couldn't stop him no matter how hard she fought.

Jason tightened his grip on her. She kicked him several times. As he walked down the road, he hit her. She bit him. He screamed, pulling one hand away, not letting go. He grumbled about the pain.

By the time they got to the stolen car, Tiffany had exhausted all the fight within her. He tied her up and tossed her into the trunk. She would not get to ride shotgun.

Tiffany tried to scream through her gag, crying out for Victor, or anyone to help her, but to no avail. Jason did not wish to take any chances. Before he closed the trunk, he gave one final blow to the side of her face, rendering her unconscious.

He drove to the dirt road that went under the bridge by the river. Dawn had shown its first glimpses. He abandoned the car, took Tiffany out of the trunk, threw her over his shoulder and carried her. They went somewhere few in the world knew existed.

He could have his way with her, torture her, and she could

scream all she wanted. No one would ever hear her cries way out in the swampy woods by the Alabaha River basin. With Victor dead in the collapse of his hidden fortress, Jason could stretch this out as long as he wanted. No one would ever know. They would search, but she would remain a missing person, a picture on the side of a milk carton.

Chapter Ten

Victor made his choice, or so he thought, but he had yet to act upon it. Living the life of a human for several weeks made him realize he did indeed enjoy having his love returned instead of having to keep it, as well as himself, hidden from his beloved. He wished to remain a human being, but now he found himself trapped. Because of that trap, he had no other choice. In order to live, he had to become an angel again. Also, after the revelation given to him by Gabriel, how could he choose anything else? His choice became no choice at all.

In an unknown place, Tiffany cried for help. The only one in the world who could help her lay trapped under a mountain of rubble, choking on the particles of dust. The largest problem did not lie because Jason had trapped Victor, but that he still held the form of a seventeen-year-old boy. A human boy would never find his way out of the rubble. Even if he crawled his way out, he'd never survive a demon such as Jason. As a Human. But an angel would have no problem. So he had no choice. Remain human and die, while allowing Tiffany to die or return to being an angel, escape from the cave-in and rush to Tiffany's aid.

Although Victor was in all parts human, he remained an angel. The only way for him to remain human was by choosing to give up what he used to be. The choice of no choice had been made. The healing process was complete. Victor would return to his formal glory.

———

Raul tried to free Victor, to no avail.

When he went to speak with the angels about Victor's plan, he asked what he could do in case of this emergency. They forbade him to do anything with his powers, unless Victor took his angelic form again. This shows the helpless pain of every Watcher. Watching the human make catastrophic mistakes, knowing what to do to help, yet unable to do anything.

Something happened that broke Raul's chain of thought and plastered a smile upon his face and joy in his heart. He knew he would get to see his friend in action again.

The surrounding debris shook and Victor's body glowed as he had once again become that which he had so hoped to abandon forever. Victor made the mistake of trying to do things his way instead of God's way. With the roar of a lion, he reared back his head, spread his arms wide, and his wings popped from behind him. He grew to over nine feet tall. He was still in solid form, but now fully angelic with all the powers.
"Raaaarrrrrggghhh!" he cried again and leaped from his rubble grave, throwing the pile around him and flew into the sky, leaving a cloud of dust in his wake. He knew where to find Tiffany, because he knew Jason. He went after Tiffany and thought he knew where she would be. So he hoped.

As soon as he had become an angel again, Gabriel went home. With a quick nod and a wink to Raul, Gabriel left.

When Victor arrived at the cabin, he found evidence that Jason had been there. It hadn't been long since he left. Victor knew he would soon return and that his time, the time he needed to find Tiffany and rescue her, grew short. He rushed into the cabin, ripping the door from its rusty hinges, and found Tiffany curled in the corner tied up; weak, beaten and stricken with fear, shaking and weeping. She buried her face deep into her arms. As he stepped closer, she recoiled in fear.

Fear! Something he never thought he would see in her again. It filled her essence and the surrounding air. Every breath thickened the blood-curdling aura of horror that filled the room. The thought of his beloved Tiffany lying there, wrapped in such terror that it emitted into the air, angered him. What had that monster done to her? With gentle steps, Victor walked over to her, and his angelic heart ached with the pain of every labored step. He kneeled in front of her and an arrow of pain pierced his heart as she again pulled herself back, although she could cower no further.

He reached out to her and touched her arm, and she looked up. Jason had beaten her. Both eyes had bruises with one swollen shut. Hand marks formed bruises around her neck and on her arms from being choked and man–or demon–handled. Her mouth had dried blood around it, making it appear as if she had grown a beard of blood. Bruises had risen behind and around her ears. Her hair appeared as if someone had been continually pulling her head back or leading her around with it. She was hardly recognizable. If it hadn't been for her blue eyes, Victor may have not recognized her.

"Haven't you done enough already?" Tears streamed from her eyes. This ripped the heart out of Victor's chest. He could imagine someone holding it, still beating in their hand and squeezing. He looked at her with complete compassion.

"It's okay," he replied in a soft voice as he swallowed back his tears for, he had indeed seen terror in Tiffany's eyes. He could not hide the pain that he suffered for her and the compassion, a strange mixture that it was, within his own eyes. "It's me," he said in a loving voice and smile. "Victor will make everything alright."

At first, she didn't recognize him. She had never seen him in his full angelic excellence and beauty. When he smiled, she looked into his eyes and knew him as Victor. Peace came over her as she knew her rescuer had come. Then, as she looked past Victor at the open door, her slight smile faded and her fear returned. As Victor saw her face, he knew Jason stood behind him.

"So, you decided not to forsake your heritage after all." He sneered, "Good, then it will be a fair fight. I've been looking forward to this moment for weeks." He turned his head to each side, popping the spine in his neck while keeping his overconfident gaze.

"Don't worry." Victor winked at Tiffany, who was stunned with fear. "I'll be right back to set you free. Let me take care of this insignificant problem first." He slowly stood and as he leisurely turned toward Jason, the peaceful smile left his face and turned to a stern gaze of contempt that would drop the weakest foes.

"Today," he said as he walked toward Jason, "is your last day on this earth. Tiffany will be the last person you will ever torment. Today, I am sending you to hell." Victor rose to his full splendor, and all of his power had completely returned. He was once again completely angel and was near his full strength.

Jason was no fool. He knew Victor outmatched him. So, he hoped to take advantage of being more familiar with the territory. As Victor stalked toward him, Jason started talking junk, "You should have died as a human when that building collapsed on you." He backed out of the door. "How did you survive that, anyway?" He walked faster, not taking his eyes off of Victor for a second. *Just a little further,* he thought, *keep following me a little further.* He backed up some more, and Victor kept skulking onward. "I know you couldn't turn into an angel before. How did you do it?" He was stalling. Victor kept stalking toward him, staring holes through him.

"Ah, c'mon, it won't hurt you to give a little answer, would it?" Victor didn't answer. *A little further,* Jason thought, his gaze never leaving Victor's. "Was it… oh, what's his name… Rowell, no… uh, Russell, no… Raul, that's it. Was it Raul that saved your sorry butt?" Victor still didn't respond, and kept walking and staring. *Only two more steps, you big colossal idiot, and you'll be in my trap.* "It was Raul, wasn't it?"

Victor stopped just short of the booby trap Jason wished to spring, and spoke, still holding his fearsome gaze at Jason, "You forget," his voice held a stern tone, "God is on my side. Apparently, he's not ready for me yet. Maybe he has sent me to be your executioner. You have been judged, and you have been awaiting your sentence since that time. I'm here now to…"

"Oh, c'mon, really?" Jason interrupted, "cut the monologue already. I'm supposed to be the bad guy here, that's my job." He laughed and then continued doing his best mocking imitation of

Victor. "'I'm your executioner.' Get a life."

With lightning-fast reflexes Victor leaped from the doorway and plowed into Jason, avoiding the trap that had Jason had set for him, grabbing him and flying straight up into the sky pulling some negative G's that would make the most seasoned fighter pilot lose his lunch. Within seconds, he had Jason thousands of feet in the air.

"Let me go!" he screamed, "Let me go!" He kept screaming, so when Victor got to a certain height, he stopped and that is exactly what he did; he let go. Jason, a demon and ghoul, may have had many powers, (magic, persuasion, haunting, the dark arts, sorcery or pharmacological talents), but the one thing that he didn't have was wings.

Flailing and screaming, he went crashing toward the ground at one hundred and twenty miles per hour. Just before he hit the ground, Victor swooped in to catch him. He wrapped him in a constrictor grip that took his breath away, let loose and did it again. He did this three more times. The last time he caught Jason, turned and slammed him into the ground. The impact made a crater. He swooped and smashed with an elbow drop that would make any professional wrestler proud. Finally, he flew back up and landed right next to him, standing victoriously over the crumpled body of Jason, the demon ghoul.

Just that quick, Victor was the victor. Jason didn't even have the time to spring any of the traps he set for this occasion. He didn't have time to call his demon brothers. They wouldn't have come, anyway; demons often just look out for themselves and don't care about any others. After standing over Jason and staring for a moment, Victor remembered Tiffany. He went to the cabin to set her free.

"I told you I'd be back, didn't I?" he smiled as she smiled back and it obviously hurt for her to do so, and to laugh, which she did and then recoiled in pain. Victor untied her and as soon as she could she embraced him and cried and tried to talk through the blubbering.

"I thought he would get me again, and I thought I was dead.

Thought you were dead. I–I–I'm glad you came for me." She pulled back from him and looked him over one good time. "So, does this mean that you can't stay, or stay as a human?"

"I'll always be here, sweet. You just won't see me anymore. I'm not leaving, I never will; I'm going to disappear for a while." His face was sad at this, and she understood.

With that understanding, she grabbed him and gave him a good long embrace one more time while she still could, "I'm going to miss you."

"Yes, I know, and I will also miss you, but I guess it wouldn't have been good for us, anyway. It's better this way, really." Victor didn't want to let go because he knew he would never hold her in his arms ever again. Tiffany let go with a gasp. The fear that struck her eyes told him everything that he needed to know about why she backed away, wagging her head. No time for him to react, only to turn.

Jason had dragged himself back into the cabin as Tiffany and Victor were having their moment and had gotten himself back to his feet. He held a large steel pipe above his head and he had taken every ounce of energy that he had left in his limp body for one final plunge at his nemesis and if this blow went where it was aimed it would be the final day for Victor, the Watcher and Warrior angel of God. As he stabbed, Raul, who had been watching over the situation, solidified and as Raul did that, he swung with his sword of truth, slicing Jason through the midsection. The iron pipe dropped to the ground with a clang and. The two halves of Jason flopped to the ground with a sickening thud.

This happened within the time that Victor realized, turned, and shrugged enough to avoid the impact. This exercise would have proven useless as the thrust of Jason was sure to hit the mark.

Before he could say, "whoa," it was all over, and Raul had sheathed his sword, smiling at his old friend. Tiffany ducked to the ground and pulled to be safe. The shock was obvious on her face as Raul broke the silence.

"Everyone okay?" His smile broadened. They nodded their

response as they stared at the rapid decay of the body of Jason. Within seconds, the body burst into flames and burned to a black powder. Without even a puff of smoke, Jason was gone.

Tiffany came to her senses and with her best inquisitive gaze, she asked, cocking her head to one side, "And you are?"

Tossing his head back, Raul replied with a roaring laugh and then said, "I'm Raul. Like Victor, I'm a Watcher angel… well, sort of."

"What do you mean, 'sort of'?" Her stare had widened, but remained.

He laughed again, "Yes, I can see why Victor adores you so." Still smiling, he continued, "I was a Watcher long ago, but I have been a trainer since, well, that is except for the past few weeks."

"So, you're Victor's boss?"

"No," he said, still laughing, "more like a mentor and a friend."

Victor gained his senses. "Wait a minute, 'the last couple of weeks'? Have you been watching over me?"

"Well, somebody had to keep you alive long enough to come to your senses. I've been watching over Tiffany too." Raul had placed his hand on Victor's shoulder. "I'm glad you're back, though."

Tiffany's smile broadened, and she said, with a special gleam in her eye, smug countenance and a confident nod, "Well, look at me. I knew I had a fan club of guys, and now I've even got two angels watching me." All they could do was laugh.

Victor's smile remained fixed as he looked at Tiffany with his own glint in his eye, "That's my Tiffany," he nodded, "That's my girl."

Raul disappeared and Tiffany ran to embrace Victor before he too went away. He looked at Tiffany with a smile. Slowly pushing her away, he said, "I must go now."

"I know," she smiled. Victor faded away, never to be seen by her again.

Chapter Eleven
Epilogue

After taking Tiffany to the hospital and telling all that he knew to the sheriff, Victor left.Later, Raul came for Victor, who sat on the edge of a small cloud, meditating. "It's time, my old friend," Raul broke the silence.

Victor sighed, "Yes, we must get the inquisition over with." He paused without breaking his gaze from the Colorado River. "Do you think they will let me stay with her?" Raul could see the pain of realization in Victor's eyes. He knew the answer to his own question. Raul shook his head.

"I don't." He knew Victor didn't need an answer. "When the angel council ends, I have a perfect assignment befitting your special talents. A young lady that needs you more than even Tiffany did."

Victor returned his gaze to the scene below. "Will I ever see her again?"

Raul smiled, sticking out his hand to aid his friend to rise. "It's a small world. Come on, let's get this over with."

***

70 years later.

Tiffany lay in the bed at the hospital, weak and dying, surrounded by her family, four children, two sons and two daughters. With them, their families, which gave her twelve grandchildren, who had given her three great grandchildren. It was a wonderful family and an awesome legacy for her to leave. Also in the room, although unseen by all, stood her Watcher angel and the watcher angels of the others, for they were all children of God. She brought them all to the Lord through the church. Raised them on the power of the Word of God. They brought it to their children and their children to theirs and on down the line.

One of her sons was a minister, the pastor of a small congregation. One of her daughters was a war hero, decorated with the bronze star and many other medals of valor. A couple of her grandsons were now serving their country, while others also served their God in the church. Her legacy could be seen in her family to the third generation, and those who would live in her influence. She was a remarkable woman who had fought a tough fight. The time had come for her to be offered. Her family gathered around her, as many as could come to her in her final moments to honor her life.

She had shared her wisdom and even told stories of her struggles in the past. Now they all gathered as if she, their great matriarch, could show just one last light of wisdom before the Lord took her home. There was one story she told no one and would now take to her grave. It was the story of her angel, Victor, the one who kept her alive.

Her breathing slowed to the point to where she barely breathed at all. Then she said something everyone in that room would always ponder. Only Raul and one other unseen visitor knew what it meant. But because she took the story to her grave, no one else ever would. They would just wonder for the rest of their lives what it meant. With her final intake of breath, she opened her big, still exquisite eyes wide with recognition, smiled, and as she released that very last breath she said one word: "Victor!" She faded away with a smile on her face.

Acknowledgements

I would like to thank all those who aided me during completing this book. Thanks to my wonderful wife, Lisa, for putting up with me as I slowly churned through this thing. Thanks to God, my King, for allowing me the pleasure of creating life.

About the Author: David Amburgey lives in Metro Atlanta, Georgia with his family where he works on his writings, and works with the local church.

Thank you for reading. God Bless.